The Trouble With Unicorns

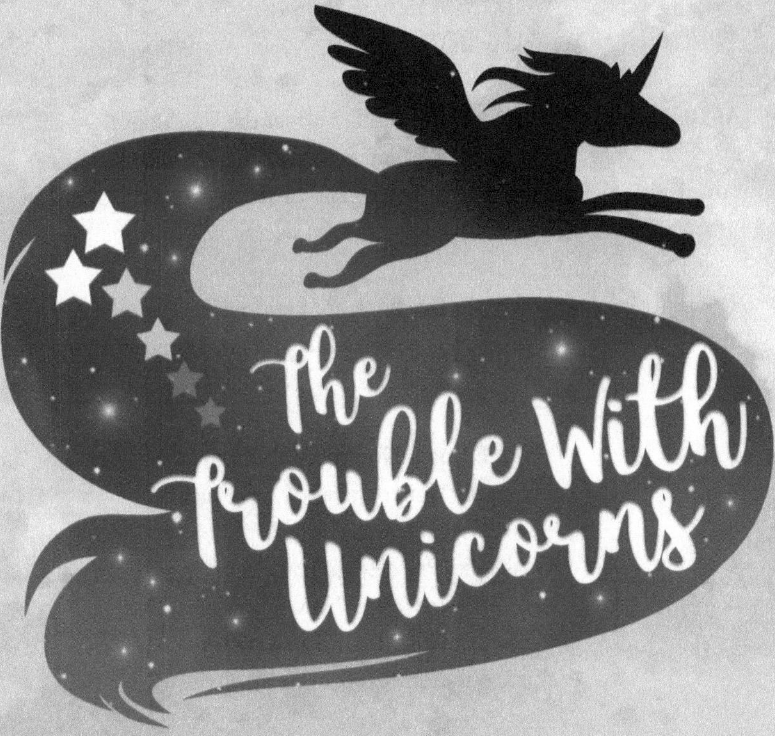

AVA WIXX

First Edition: November 2025
Published in the United States of America by
Wicked Wixx Press.
The Wicked Wixx Press Logo is a trademark of
Wicked Wixx Press.
Originally published under the title
The Trouble with Unicorns: 2018

Cover Art, Ava Wixx Logo, Wicked Wixx Logo, Team Unicorn Talia
Logo & Interior Book Graphics by Lindsay Tiry of LT Arts
Edited by Melissa Ringsted of There for You Editing

Print ISBN: 978-1-955950-51-0
Kindle ISBN: 978-1-955950-52-7
EPUB ISBN: 978-1-955950-53-4

For more information visit: avawixx.com

*Until I married one, I never appreciated the true power
optimists wield.
This one is for all you optimists out there ...
You're stronger than you get credit for.*

#1

Chapter 1

"**D**on't leave me!" I was dragged across the linoleum floor as I grappled with the massive dragon warrior, my nails digging into his leather-clad leg.

Halting, Daegus bent over, a scowl tugging his lips down even as his green eyes danced with mirth. "Now, do you really think this is going to work?" He shook his tree trunk of a leg, and I slid down past his kneecap, my face scant inches from the black and white checkers.

"This is why I need you! Because, yes, I actually thought I could force you to stay by clinging to you like a friggin' spider monkey."

Daegus tapped the tip of my nose with his callused index finger. "No you didn't."

I blinked at him balefully. "Would it help if I cried?"

He chuckled. "Absolutely not."

Sighing, I released him, flopping over onto my back. "What am I going to do without you?"

Closing my eyes, I considered my current predicament. As a unicorn shifter, the rare gem the name implied, I, along with others of my kind, were protected by Daegus' family. Somewhere along the line in our shared history, Daegus' ancestors had sworn a protection oath to my ancestors ... blabbity, blah, blah. The bottom line was: I'd been raised by Daegus after my parents had been slaughtered by demons, their deaths a perceived failure on his part. Now a week after my thirtieth birthday, it was time for a changing of the guards, so to speak. Daegus, an ancient dragon, had stepped in to take responsibility for me, but it had been decided that I would receive my permanent guardian at thirty, just like tradition mandated. The problem was, I didn't want Daegus to go. Nor did I want to be strapped with some dragon I didn't know, one who was supposed to help me on my demon tracking missions, aka the one who would do all the stabby things since I balked at the sight of blood. But I couldn't help it, unicorns simply didn't carry the badass gene. We excelled at other things—things that didn't require me to figure out how to remove red cells, platelets, and all that disgusting mess of goo from my clothes.

Groaning, I rolled over onto my stomach, and pushed myself to my feet. I swayed, grabbing at the wall, finding Daegus' steady chest instead. My fingers curled against his leather breastplate. My eyes rolled reflexively. No matter how many times I thrust a current calendar in his face, my dragon-of-a-father-figure was convinced we were still living in ancient times where head-to-toe leather was worn by warriors, and not just people with fetishes.

I shoved away from my antiquated dragon. "But what if this new dragon isn't good at dealing with demons? What if he gets me killed? What if he—"

Daegus pulled me against him, kissing the top of my head with affection. His familiar spicy scent surrounded and comforted me. "Now, where did my little optimist go? It isn't like you to worry so much about something like this."

Pulling away from him, I glowered. "Just because I'm an optimist doesn't mean I'm Little Miss Sunshine all the time, as you well know. I have genuine concerns about this new dragon." I crossed my arms over my chest, and glared up at the male who'd raised me, my left eye twitching.

He ran his hands through his shoulder-length auburn hair, his expression remaining placid. "Talia, we've talked about this at length. It's time for you to receive your permanent guardian—"

"But I never agreed! I don't understand why you can't be my permanent guardian! We work so well together, and—"

"I was never meant to stay here forever. It's time for me to move on."

"Don't you love me?" My lower lip quivered.

Daegus barked out a laugh, his head falling back.

"Don't pull that crap on me. I told you tears wouldn't work, and neither will emotional manipulation. The new dragon is coming. Deal with it."

"You're so mean," I huffed. "Maybe I won't miss you after all."

He swiped a freshly frosted cupcake from the kitchen counter, popping the whole thing into his mouth, his cheeks puffing out. My baking spree had been another attempt at convincing him to stay. It had failed, too. Although he was apparently more than happy to eat my astoundingly good pastries despite that fact. "Hey! Only dragons who don't abandon the unicorn they swore to always be there for get to eat the cupcakes."

Daegus lifted an eyebrow, snatching several of the sugar cookies instead. They had little dragon and unicorn designs on them, meant to remind him that we were a team. I lunged, hissing, "Cookies either!" Dancing back and forth in front of the counter, I smacked at his hands. "None for you! They're for the new dragon you insist is coming."

"You can give him the shirt. I'll take these." Daegus swooped to the right, grabbing the entire pan of cupcakes, and sifted ... there one moment, gone the next. *Typical dragon maneuver.*

"Not fair!" I shook my fist at the empty space. When he didn't reappear, I shifted from foot to foot. "Are you at least going to come back and say a proper good-bye?" I swallowed around the lump in my throat. We'd discussed a lot of things, but not when I'd see him again, or how I could get a hold of him in case of an emergency. Was he actually going to cut and run, leaving me without any answers ... or even a phone number? "Coward!"

"Excuse me?" a deep, unfamiliar voice rumbled.

Spinning, my right foot tangled with my left, and I toppled forward. Strong arms caught me around the waist, propping me against the kitchen counter. Blowing a piece of aqua-tinted hair out of my face, I glanced up to find— *Holy crap! This cannot be the new dragon! He's—he's ...* My mind blanked, even as my eyes drank him in.

It was difficult to tell how old he was, since dragons aged so ridiculously slow that they were practically immortal. I was guessing about mid-thirties, give or take a few decades. Dark, rumpled hair framed a masculine, angular face. Bright blue eyes scanned my features as my gaze dipped to survey his sculpted body. Even in jeans and a T-shirt the ridges of his muscles were visible. And he was tall to boot, towering over my willowy height of 5'10". I resisted the urge to fan myself. *Hot damn, he is one massive specimen of manly deliciousness. Maybe I really won't miss Daegus after all.*

I shook my head. *No. That's not right. I can't think of him that way. He's going to be my partner. Just because Daegus didn't let me date, like ever, doesn't mean I have to go crazy over the first delectable supernatural creature to cross my path the second he's gone.*

But it's not like I'm a virgin ... much to Daegus' chagrin. My dragon protector had found that out the hard way when he'd stumbled upon me and a devastatingly sexy light fae, naked and … experimenting. The incident had ended with said fae, terrified and high-tailing it into the woods, with a pissed off dragon hot on his heels, wielding a flaming sword. That particular incident had promptly halted all interest from the fae community in me. They were curious creatures, drawn by all things beautiful, which as I unicorn I definitely was … but apparently they weren't that curious. Daegus had been pleased. Me … not so much.

I shook my head again, dispelling the memory.

Then it hit me … dark hair. Jet-black in fact. I cleared my throat, forcing my gaze up. "Umm … you're a water dragon?" It came out as a question, but I already knew the answer. I wasn't an expert on dragons, but I'd picked up on a few things since I'd been raised by one. It wasn't as if Daegus had been forthcoming on information about all the dragon clans—he'd mostly focused on his own—but I did know that the color of a dragon's hair in human form indicated what type he or she was. And black hair meant water dragon … not fire dragon like my father figure.

A frown twisted the new dragon's full lips. "Yeah, I'm a water dragon. I thought you were expecting me?"

The tips of my ears heated. "Well, yes, I was expecting my new and permanent guardian, but Daegus didn't tell me a thing about you. Not even your name."

"So you thought I'd be a fire dragon—"

"Like Daegus, and his family. How is it even possible— " I snapped my mouth shut, not wanting to be rude. Smoothing my hands down the front of my long dress, I attempted to gather my thoughts. Every type of dragon had the ability to wield fire, but none as powerful as a red dragon, aka fire dragon. A black dragon, aka water dragon, held dominion over water. The thing was ... *How the hell is a water dragon part of a fire dragon family?* I'd been under the impression that the different clans didn't intermingle much. My left eye twitched. I was missing something.

I cleared my throat. "Like I was saying, Daegus didn't even tell me your name ..." I raised my eyebrows, waiting.

"Bryn. Bryn O'Bannon. And I'm not just a dragon, I'm ... well, half something else. Our queen, the dragon queen, had me sent to my adoptive parents when I was just a baby. Insisted I be raised by them, and trained to become your guardian one day. It's why a black dragon like me ended up in a family of red dragons."

Well, now that's interesting. Very interesting indeed. Not only is he a black dragon raised by red dragons, but he has a full human name, and not a complicated name like his kind tended to favor. Daegus was short for something long, and practically unpronounceable. But Bryn O'Bannon was ... I had to know more, even if it was impolite to pry. "What's the something else? And what interest does the dragon queen have in you?" *Or me for that matter.* Leaning back on my elbows, I stared up at him, drumming my fingers across the granite.

He snorted. "It's none of your business. Not sure why I even brought it up."

I pointed at myself. "Unicorn. People like to open up to

me. Some can't help it." I grinned, hoping it would encourage him to divulge more information about himself. After all, we were going to be partners. The more we knew about each other, the better. At least that's the way I saw it.

Crossing his arms over his sculpted chest, his gaze skimmed over the confectionary goodness scattered across the counter. His nostrils flared. "You bake those for me?"

My lower lip jutted out into a pout. "Kind of."

He skirted around me, scooping up several cookies and shoving them into his mouth without even stopping to appreciate the designs I'd taken the time to adorn them with. Crumbs falling from his lips, he muttered, "Not bad. You cook often?"

"That depends. You going to finish telling me about yourself?"

"I told you all you need to know." He stuffed two more cookies into his mouth, his jaw muscles rippling as he chewed.

"Then no, I don't cook often." Truth was, I enjoyed baking. It soothed my nerves. Plus, I liked feeding the neighborhood kids, and animals. I even had an awesome recipe for peanut butter dog treats. I also made nut clusters for the squirrels and chipmunks. Sharing free food garnered goodwill like nothing else could, and it was in my nature to want to make others happy.

But none for Bryn!

"Shame." Gathering another handful of cookies, he

glanced over his shoulder towards the staircase. "So, where's my room?"

"Second floor, end of the hall—" Before I could even finish my sentence he had sifted away. *Typical dragon.* Not that I'd known many. Just Daegus, and a few of his family members who'd visited over the years. But the popping in and out unannounced, plus the way he'd stuffed his face with my pastries unapologetically ... all things I'd become accustomed to living with Daegus.

Flopping into a chair, I thumped my forehead against the kitchen table. *Daegus is gone, and Bryn is here to stay.* I needed to make the best of it. Maybe Bryn was just as flustered by the new situation as I was. I'd simply have to try harder with him, make an effort to welcome him better.

Grabbing the shirt I'd made for Daegus, the one he'd clearly not wanted, I plastered a smile on my face and sprinted up the stairs. *Ready or not, Mr. Bryn O'Bannon, we're about to start the journey to becoming lifelong friends.*

Chapter 2

Unicorns are associated with being unique, magical … special. I translate that to mean singular, weird … alone. Not that I didn't have a plethora of humans and creatures of all origins that were constantly surrounding me, but none of them knew the real me. They couldn't. It would eventually result in my death. Just like with my parents. Somewhere along the line they must have trusted the wrong person, setting their untimely demise into motion. It was why the few of us remaining were spread out over the world, hidden even from each other. Demons, vampires, warlocks, even some breeds of particularly nasty dark fae would do near anything to get their hands on any part of a unicorn … blood, skin, and especially the horn. Thankfully, most still believed us a myth or extinct, which was fine by me.

Except … well, for the whole lonely thing.

Daegus had been my father figure, sure, but he had

also held the position of my best friend. His clan, or family, were the only beings in any dimension who knew what I truly was, but it wasn't like I got to interact with them on a daily basis, if at all. Which was exactly why Bryn was going to be more than my mere guardian. He would be my partner in crime, my confidant, and my friend. I wasn't giving him a choice. *In the end, I'm sure he'll thank me. After all, who doesn't want a unicorn for a BFF?*

Then again, Daegus couldn't get out of here fast enough. I shook my head. *No.* Daegus simply missed his kind. Since serving as my guardian, he'd been isolated as well. I knew it hadn't been easy for the ancient warrior to be sequestered away with a unicorn for the past three decades. I was like a daughter to him, but I knew he had longings, one of which was to find his *Anam Cara*, the dragon equivalent of a mate. From what I understood the pairing took 'until death do us part' to a whole new level.

I internally squealed. *Maybe someday soon I'll have little Daegus' running around for me to play with and spoil. Hmm ... they'd be my siblings ... sort of.*

Okay. Stop thinking about babies and focus on making Bryn want to be your friend.

Lifting my chin, I glided down the hallway, my cheeks aching from the grin plastered across my face. My eyes narrowed on Bryn's frozen form just outside his bedroom. A large duffle bag rested against the wall at his feet. *What the hell is he doing?* Clearing my throat, I opened my mouth to speak.

He swung around, scrubbing a hand along his jaw. "This is a joke, right?"

Halting, I tilted my head, taking in his bewildered expression. "What's a joke? Don't you like your room?"

A choking sound escaped his throat. "It looks like a damn rainbow threw up in there."

"I happen to like bright colors!"

His eyebrows lifted. "Are you planning on staying in there with me?"

"What? No, of course not. I—"

"Then I'm changing it."

My face warmed, and I swallowed back annoyance. Bryn probably preferred dark colors like Daegus. *Sigh. Dragons. Or is it just males?* But he had every right to make his room look whatever way he liked. I'd simply wanted it to be inviting. Obviously my definition and his were different. "Fine, whatever. Change what you want. It's your room." My lips stretched with effort across my teeth, pulling up into another smile. "Here," I shoved the shirt at him, "I want you to have this."

He snatched the white material from my grasp, holding it up in front of himself. "What—what the hell is this?"

Pursing my lips, I said, "I think it's pretty obvious what it is."

Flipping the shirt around, he showed me the design I already knew was there. In the middle of the white cotton was a circle with a blue cloud background within it. Set against the background, in the center of the circle, was a chibi-style unicorn head with *Team Unicorn Talia* printed on the top and bottom, separated by two hearts, one on each side. It was an adorable little logo I had made up to remind Daegus whose 'team' he was on. But since he didn't want it, I thought it was a good gift for Bryn instead. You know, to welcome him to the partnership he was now officially bound to. My team. Team Unicorn Talia. *Go me!*

Chuckling, I bounced up onto the balls of my feet, and clapped. "It's adorable, I know!"

"But … what's it mean?"

I rolled my eyes, and pointed at myself. "Me, Talia. Me, unicorn. You're on my team now as my partner and guardian. So Team Unicorn Talia. Get it?"

"You want me to wear this or something?"

"Only out on missions. I mean, I wouldn't want the demons to get confused about whose side you're on."

Bryn's jaw muscles flexed as his nostrils flared, no words forthcoming. His baby blues bore into me with uncertainty.

Snatching the shirt back, I poked his chest with my index finger. "It was a joke. At least the part about wearing it out on missions. But clearly you don't want the shirt so I'll just take it back." *Ungrateful, rude, moody … asshat!*

"Wait. I—" He ran a hand through his midnight locks, swallowing hard. "Look, I'm sorry. Even though I've been training since practically birth to be your guardian, this is all a bit ... disconcerting. I didn't really know what to expect when it came to you as an individual. And you're, " he waved his hand in my general direction, "a lot to take in."

I stared down at the Team Unicorn Talia logo. "I do have a tendency to be a little over the top about things." I lifted my gaze to meet his, my lips twitching. "The shirt's a bit much, huh?"

One corner of his mouth tugged up. "Yeah, just a little. I am a dragon warrior, after all. We don't usually wear cartoon logos on our shirts, especially when out hunting demons."

I pictured Bryn donning the shirt while on a mission. I internally giggled, the mental image extremely pleasing to me. "Well, you'd be a lot cooler if you did." I cleared my throat, and shook my head, bringing myself back to reality. "I guess that's why Daegus didn't want it either."

He grinned, a dimple popping out on each cheek. "Probably."

"Okay, well, I guess I won't make the big bad dragon warrior wear the cutesy unicorn shirt."

"Thanks, I appreciate it," he deadpanned.

A chill raced up my spine, goose bumps erupting in quick succession along my skin. Gasping for breath, I fought to swallow the bile that erupted up my esophagus, threatening to suffocate me.

"Talia." Bryn's voice was far away, as if I was hearing it through a tunnel. His eyes glowed as they focused on me, dancing back and forth in assessment. "Tell me what's wrong." Strong arms slid under my shoulders and behind my knees, lifting.

I tried to form the words to respond, but I knew it was useless. The sensations I was experiencing were familiar, and although they weren't welcome, I'd come to accept them.

"Talia, please. Tell me what to do."

Darkness pushed around the edges of my vision, stealing Bryn's beautiful visage. I whimpered, not wanting to face what I knew was inevitable.

Images … images too horrible for me to comprehend skidded across my brain, forcing themselves upon me. I concentrated on focusing past those, past the death and mayhem, past the anger and fear, to what I needed to find.

Ah, there you are. There's the demon. I snatched the imprint of its energy, settling it into my core so I'd never forget. Now I could find it anywhere.

I smiled to myself before wrenching out of Bryn's arms, landing awkwardly on my feet, and ejecting the contents of my stomach all over his duffle bag. *Fabulous.*

Blinking up at Bryn, I wiped my mouth with the back of my hand. "Sorry," I muttered. "But the good news is we have our first demon to track." I straightened up, groaning as I rubbed my temples. "But first I'm going to go brush my teeth real quick." I considered the way my hair clung to my cheeks and neck. "Or maybe a shower. Meet me downstairs in ten, and be ready to battle a demon!"

Dashing down the hall to my room, I slammed the door behind me, not waiting for Bryn's reaction. Although embarrassing to have thrown up on my soon to be BFF's duffle bag, my mood buoyed. After all, it was a good sign from the universe that our first hunt was already under way. It told me that our partnership was truly meant to be. I grinned. *Yep. This is the beginning of something beautiful. I just know it.*

Chapter 3

The thing about being an optimist is that we see the world differently than most. It doesn't mean we avoid the ugly truth of reality, or when faced with horrible things we don't accept them. It simply means that no matter how many times we get knocked down, we will find a way to get back on our feet, and be grateful for the second or billionth chance. We're not stupid, or even naïve. We just believe that positive conquers negative, and therefore staying positive is the only sure-fire way to win at the game called life.

Although I will admit, my sense of seeing the silver lining wasn't always appreciated. Especially by moody dragon warriors by the name of Bryn.

"Can you please stop grinning like you're deranged? Less than twenty minutes ago you were so repulsed by the energy of a demon you tossed your cookies all over my stuff."

Bouncing in my seat, I pointed to the right. "That way. You need to go that way." The center of my forehead burned, letting me know we were going in the right direction. If I was in my other form, my horn would be glowing brightly as I tracked.

Bryn gave me some major side eye before following my directions, and swinging the minivan to the right. "Seriously, why are you so happy?"

Tilting my head, I considered him. "I guess it's because I feel most alive when I'm helping people … balancing the scales towards the good side of things."

Bryn's fingers tapped along the steering wheel. "So why don't you just go out and eradicate all of the evil in the world? Stop all the shitty things humans do, too? Doesn't it bother you when you see stuff in the news about all the hate and—"

I waved my hands about. "That line of thinking is dangerous, no matter how well placed your intentions are. Light can't exist without dark. There must be balance. What if the sun never set? What if we never had rainy days? What if no one ever died? This world, and all worlds for that matter, exist because of balance. It's simply my job to make sure the dark doesn't overtake the light. Think about it …" I turned my gaze out the window. "The brighter the light, the darker the shadow it casts. Before, when I got … ill from sensing the demon's energy, it's not because it's evil per say, and I'm the epitome of good." I shook my head. "No, that's not it at all. I just had a violent reaction because our vibes are diametrically opposed.

We're opposites and we repel on a base level. But in the end, light and dark must always co-exist, neither can be destroyed without resulting in the end of everything."

"Does the demon sense you?"

"It senses something, but it's not the same for them."

"And if it would mean the end of everything, then why do demons continue to try to wipe out good?"

I laughed. "Because they're myopic and just don't get it —they don't see the bigger picture. Or at least that's my theory."

Bryn glanced at me, his lips twisting down. "I'm not so sure I understand any of this myself. I mean, I was trained in what I'm supposed to do, but ..."

Reaching over, I placed my hand on his forearm. He flinched away. "It's okay. I'll help you understand."

His only response was a grunt.

The burning in the center of my forehead intensified, and I swung my head to the left and then right, narrowing my gaze against the pressure. "We're getting closer. I can feel it."

"Which way?"

"Just keep going straight." I nodded to myself.

"So how ..." Bryn cleared his throat. "How do you know when the scales are balanced?"

I scrunched up my nose. Whoever had trained him must have concentrated heavily on the brawn part, because he was seriously lacking in knowledge. I eyed his muscular arms. *Not that I'm complaining.* Forcing my gaze up to his chiseled profile, I answered, "When I stop sensing demons for a while that means the scales are balanced. Sort of. Obviously all unicorns don't sense the same demons. We don't, because otherwise, every demon I tracked would have a bunch of us on its tail. I'm honestly not sure how that part works. Why I sense some and not others. The scales always feel balanced to me when I take care of the demon I sensed, it's hard to describe." I shrugged. "But when I'm done with a case, until another demon blips on my radar I do other things." I tucked my hair behind my ears. "Like volunteer at animal shelters, babysit ... anything to make the world a slightly better place without throwing things out of whack myself."

"Well aren't you just a ray of fucking sunshine," Bryn muttered under his breath. I wasn't sure if I was meant to hear it, and even if I wasn't, I couldn't help but take offense.

"What's your problem with me? You've been acting like a cat stuck out in the rain since you arrived."

A muscle popped in Bryn's jaw as he ground his teeth together. "I don't have a problem with you. I just—" He slammed his fist against the steering wheel. "How would you like it if you've never had a say in your own life? Since the day I was born I was set on the path to be your permanent guardian. Not that I don't think it's a noble cause, and hell, I might have chosen it on my own but—"

"It's okay. I get it. The thing is, I haven't had much of a choice either." I crossed my arms over my chest. I wasn't just saying that to placate him. I truly did understand. It wasn't like I enjoyed hiding away from the rest of the world. And when I was a kid, Daegus moved us from city to city all over the country, searching for the best spot, until we finally found what I now considered home. I'd left a lot of places and people I cared about behind over the years, definitely not by choice. Pretty much all I had to show for it in the end was a messed up accent that was part northerner, and part southerner. *I suppose it kind of suits a unicorn to have a weird way of speaking.* I shook my head. *Focus, Talia. You're on a hunt, not a trek down memory lane.*

Clearing my throat, I said, "We just have to make the best out of our circumstances with the time we have on this earth."

"You make it sound so easy," he grunted.

"It is. Accept the things you can't change, and only worry about the things you can."

"Sounds like something you'd see on a bumper sticker."

I snorted. "I think that's where I got it from."

He rolled his eyes. "Of course it is."

"Look, like I said, I get it. Your life hasn't been your own. But you're here now, and when we're not tracking demons you can actually make your own choices about your life. Do whatever you want. Pursue interests outside of demon hunting."

His brow furrowed, and silence fell over us.

I couldn't help but wonder what kind of interests someone like Bryn might have. Daegus was ancient and had weird hobbies. He'd been content remodeling the house we'd shared. Hardwood floors gleamed, and granite countertops sparkled. He'd even installed an extra-large bathtub for me in my suite so I could soak while in either of my forms. But somehow Bryn struck me as having more pent up energy. There was a wildness about him I couldn't quite put my finger on.

I stabbed my index finger against the windshield, bouncing forward in my seat. "That way, take this right."

Swearing under his breath, Bryn followed my order, the tires squealing as we swung abruptly down a narrow road.

"With all the money you have to work with, why the hell do you have this P.O.S.?"

"What? The van? Is there anything of mine you *do* like?" Glancing around the interior of Little Miss Ole Faithful, or Faith for short, I admitted she had seen better days. But Faith was still in fine condition, and I had a tendency of getting emotionally attached to things … even old vans that were a bit rusty on the outside, and maybe the inside, too.

"Here! It's here!" My arms flailed around, smacking the roof, window, and my dragon driver's massive shoulder.

Bryn slammed on the brakes, and we skidded to an abrupt halt. Leaning forward, he peered around me, his eyes widening. "We can't stay here." Pressing down on the gas, we peeled out. The force of the momentum threw me back against my seat.

"What the hell do you think you're doing? The demon was there somewhere!"

"Yeah, and did you notice where exactly we were? Huh?"

"Sure, it was a playground. Now go back." I swatted at his arm.

"And you don't see a problem with two adults pulling up to said playground, in a white windowless van, and with no children of their own?"

I crossed my arms over my chest. "Well, when you put it that way."

"Again I'm going to ask, why the hell do you have this thing?" He slapped his huge hand against the dash.

"Sometimes we might need to take a possessed soul with us so I can work on them in private. All demon hunting missions don't end in a clean kill, you know."

"Yeah, I'm well aware that not all demons are powerful enough to come to Earth in their true forms, and some can only take possession of humans. But I thought—"

"Stop thinking," I snapped. "That's my job on the hunts. Yours is to be my backup. So shut up and listen to me, damnit."

Bryn's lips quirked. "You are so not what I thought a unicorn would be like."

"What's that supposed to mean?"

He shrugged even as his lips stretched into a grin, showcasing dimples.

I resisted the urge to push the issue. It didn't matter what he thought a unicorn would be like, obviously he was undereducated when it came to my kind. "Just head to that residential area a few miles back and we can leave the van there temporarily while we borrow a car."

His eyebrows lifted. "You have friends there or something?"

"No," I huffed. "We're going to borrow an inconspicuous car to go to the playground."

"You mean steal?"

"No. We'll return it as soon as we're done using it, so borrow. Borrow. Say it with me ... borrow."

"Yep. Definitely not what I'd thought a unicorn would be like. Bright colors and sage bumper sticker advise aside."

I poked him in the shoulder with my index finger. "Just shut up and drive faster."

He chuckled, causing me to scowl.

This whole being friends thing with Bryn is going to be a lot more difficult than I'd originally thought. He's just so ... so ... prickly and annoying.

I glared at his profile, my gaze zeroing in on one of his delectable dimples.

At least he's pretty to look at.

Chapter 4

"**W**ould Daegus have let you do this?"

"Who do you think taught me?" I winked before turning my attention back to the wires under the dash of the car I'd slipped into. "The thing is, it only works with older cars, or I only know how to hot wire the older ones. New cars with all of their newfangled electronics confused Daegus, therefore me."

Bryn leaned in close in an attempt to see exactly what I was doing. His clean scent swirled around me as his hot breath fanned across my cheek. "I still can't believe the door was unlocked."

I swallowed, my throat suddenly parched. "This is Tennessee, Bryn, not New York. People are generally more trusting here."

He snorted. "Obviously they shouldn't be."

The car's engine roared to life, and a self-satisfied grin spread across my face. "Okey dokey, let's get this show on the road." Sitting up, I gripped the large steering wheel, narrowing my eyes in determination.

Leaning back in his seat, Bryn frowned. "Why do I have a bad feeling about this?"

I threw the car into reverse, backing down the slanted driveway carefully. "Because this is your first hunt with me and you're out of your element? That's just a guess though."

"Or it could be that this is my first hunt with you and I've already let you steal a car."

My ears heated as anger simmered within me. "Let me? Ha! As if you could stop me! Plus, again, I'm going to say ... borrow. I'm borrowing this car with every intention of returning it. Besides, if something does happen to it, which is highly doubtful by the way, one little car is a minor sacrifice for the safety I'm providing by disposing of the demon we're tracking. I'm sure any family would agree."

Bryn opened his mouth to reply, but I cut him off.

"Also, I'm going to say this once so you better remember it. You are not the boss of me in any way. Daegus may have been in some ways, but that was because he raised me and was—is like a father to me. You, Mr. O'Bannon, are my partner, and new to this job. You don't get to let me or tell me to do anything!" My nostrils flared. "And, you better stop being such a moody asshat because you're making it really hard to want to be friends with you." I slammed my fist against the steering wheel. "And damnit, we're going to be BFFs!"

Running through a stop sign, I turned the massive beast of a car left, heading in the direction of the playground. "Well, aren't you going to say anything in response?" I glanced at Bryn, who was staring at me slack jawed. *Shit. I've scared him off. Why am I so cranky today? I need to remember that everyone handles stress differently. Maybe he gets grumpy.* My cheeks heated with embarrassment. I was being rude. *Maybe ... should I apologize?* I warred with myself. My reaction to Bryn's moodiness was understandable, although not the right thing to do. Two wrongs never made a right. And yet, I was still annoyed at him.

A deep rumble filled the air, starting low, and escalating in volume quickly. "BFFs? She just said we're going to be BFFs."

"It's not funny," I grated, keeping my eyes glued to the road.

"Actually, yeah, it is. You've known me for what, a few hours? And you've already come to the misguided conclusion that we're going to be BFFs. If that isn't funny I don't know what is."

Slamming on the breaks, we squealed to a stop at the side of the road. "Misguided conclusion? You don't want to be friends with me?"

All mirth evaporated from Bryn, his eyes sparking

with anger. "No. I can be friendly with you, but we won't be friends. I ... I was taught to never cross that line with you."

A lump formed in my throat. "Wh-who taught you such a ridiculous thing? We're going to be partners. We're going to be—"

"We have a job to do. Being friends with you would compromise what needs to be done."

"Says who?"

"Doesn't matter," he growled. "It's a fact, so you better get used to it. I will protect you at all costs. I will serve you in all things. I will be better than a friend."

The corners of my eyes burned, and I blinked away the tears. "What could be better than a friend?"

"Me."

We stared at each other in silence, his expression stoic. Finally I decided to let it go ... temporarily. There was no way I was going to accept his stupid decree. *We will be friends, Bryn O'Bannon. Challenge friggin' accepted.* He would soon learn a unicorn's determination was far greater than a dragon's.

"Well," I cleared my throat, and threw the car into drive, "let's go get us a demon." My mood buoyed once again. I'd simply deal with Bryn and his B.S. later. For the time being I needed to focus on the task at hand.

As we sailed down the street, Bryn clutched at the dash, his complexion going ashen. "Whoa, whoa, whoa. Slow down."

"Why? We're in a hurry. We need to get to the demon before he goes somewhere else. I'm not in the mood for a long, drawn out chase." Especially because I needed to brainstorm on my grumpy dragon partner problem. I didn't have time for a complicated demon case.

"Talia, I said to slow down."

Biting my lower lip to keep from grinning, I pressed the gas pedal down to the floor.

"You need to slow down! What if you run over a kid or a dog or something?" His voice went up a few octaves.

I rolled my eyes. "Please, even in the unlikely event that I did, I'd simply heal them."

"And if you killed them?"

"I'm not killing anyone. Now calm down and act like the dragon warrior you claim to be."

"We can't speed up to the playground like this. We ... just slow the hell down, damnit!"

I tapped the brake several times, dropping our speed significantly, but keeping us going at a pretty decent clip. "And here I thought you'd be more fun than Daegus since you're not an ancient dragon like him."

"He didn't teach you how to hotwire a car, did he?" Bryn growled.

I laughed. "Of course not."

"Then where—"

"His much younger brother used to visit when I was just an itty-bitty unicorn. Showed me lots of fun things Daegus would have wrung his neck over if he knew."

"But you're a unicorn!" Bryn sputtered.

I sighed, resisting the urge to roll my eyes yet again. "I don't know why everyone expects us to be innocent, pure … and utterly boring. We're unique magical creatures who are essentially good. But having fun, getting up to a bit of mischief now and again, isn't a bad thing. It doesn't taint us in any way. In fact, it's good for the soul. Did you know demons can't laugh? At least not genuinely."

"What the hell are you talking about? Of course demons can laugh. I've seen one—"

"Nope. They can fake laugh. Mimic the emotion. But demons can never laugh in the pure sense."

"Pure sense? Once again, you've lost me."

Of course I did. He doesn't seem to understand anything. "We're here!" Throwing the car in park, I swung the door open, and jumped out, strolling towards the playground. My forehead burned, and my gut churned in anticipation. *Come out, come out wherever you are, you demon scum.*

Bryn appeared in front of me. "Talia, listen, please. We need a plan. You can't just walk around here without a child and expect—"

Placing my hand on his arm, I smiled sweetly. "Awe, Bryn. Bless your little heart. Of course I have a child." I let my gaze travel demonstratively down his massive form. "Or at least a baby dragon of sorts."

His eyes blazed, shining like twin blue flashlights. "What the hell is that supposed to mean?"

Skirting around him, I shrugged. "You figure it out. Oh, and you might want to turn off the light show. It might scare the children you seem so concerned about.

Not to mention what the parents might do." I hadn't thought about some of the added headaches having a younger dragon with me would cause. Like Bryn not being as in control of his emotions, and therefore his glowing eyes. *Ugh.*

"I like your hair." A little girl—no older than five—stood to my right, nibbling on her thumbnail. "Aqua is my favorite color, but my mommy won't let me dye it like yours."

Turning, I crouched down in front of her. "And where is your mommy?" It made me nervous that she seemed alone when there was a demon on the loose.

Ignoring my question, she stared at her blonde hair, twirling it around her finger. "I really wish she'd let me dye my hair. Tina's hair is purple. I'd settle for purple, but it's not my favorite color. Or even regular blue. Blonde is so boring."

"Honey, you need to tell me where your mommy is."

"Why?"

"So I can talk to her about you dying your hair." *And why she isn't watching you more closely, demon presence nearby or not.*

The little girl shrugged. "Don't know where my mommy is." Big blue, baleful eyes filled with tears. "But I won't cry, because I'm a big girl, and big girls don't cry."

Yanking playfully at her hair, I smiled. "That's right, you're a big girl which is why your mommy wasn't worried about you. But I'm going to help you find her now." A knot had formed in the pit of my stomach. It looked like Bryn wasn't the only one who had a bad feeling about this particular hunt. There was something ... off about it.

Grabbing her tiny hand, I stood, scanning the immediate area. Sudden heat suffused my back, hot breath caressing my ear.

"You borrowing her, too?" Bryn rumbled, his tone mocking.

Glancing over my shoulder, I noted that he'd gotten his little light show under control. "Guess you could say that." It hadn't been part of my plan, but I wasn't going to look a gift horse in the mouth.

"Now," I addressed the little girl, "where was the last place you saw your mommy?"

"Over there." She pointed towards the swings, which were now suspiciously empty.

I nodded absently, noting the pressure in my forehead increased when I faced that direction as well. *What are the chances?* Marching across the playground, I lifted my chin, keeping my senses on high alert.

"What are you?" the little girl asked.

"Huh?" I muttered.

She squeezed my hand tighter. "I asked what you were?"

"I— What?"

"Don't play stupid with me. You're not human, and you're not like anything I've ever come across before. So what are you?"

Halting abruptly, I stared down at the little girl, whose

eyes flashed red. "H-how is that possible?" *No. No. It's absolutely not possible. There is no way —*

"Talia!" Bryn bellowed.

Whirling around in confusion, I met his gaze, which was glowing again.

Everything went dark.

Chapter 5

I came to, instantly aware, but utterly confused. "What happened?" I muttered, blinking the familiar lavender of my living room ceiling into focus. My head thumped in time with my pulse as I sat up. "Bryn?"

He appeared in front of me, eyes illuminated. "How are you feeling?" He dropped to his knees, his rough hands dancing over my tender scalp.

"Ow!" I slapped at his arm. "What happened? The last thing I remember was—"

"That little girl had bodyguards. They came out of nowhere, and one of them bludgeoned you on the back of the head with a gun." Anger rippled across Bryn's features. "The demon was nowhere to be found, so I grabbed you and sifted us home. I didn't need an altercation with humans. Hopefully my glowing eyes and the fact that we disappeared into thin air won't raise too many questions." He grunted to himself, obviously worried.

"Hold up. I was pistol-whipped by a bodyguard?"

"Pretty much."

I tried to make sense of what happened, but couldn't. "But the little girl was a demon."

Bryn reached for my head again. "You sure you're feeling okay? I know unicorns heal faster than most, but maybe you need some more time to—"

Standing, I stalked into the kitchen, my stomach grumbling. I was always ravenous when my body used up energy to heal. If I was human, who knows how badly that so-called bodyguard would have injured me. "I said I'm fine. And I'm not delusional. That little girl was a demon. Which, okay, seems weird, since I didn't sense her at the playground when I had a lock on the demon before ... but her eyes flashed red. And who the hell goes around pistol-whipping people without any information? I've heard of shooting first and asking questions later, but pistol-whipping first? Really?"

Biting into a stack of sugar cookies, I chewed while reviewing the facts. I'd tracked the demon to the playground like normal, but that's when things went wonky. The little girl had been touching me, and I'd sensed absolutely nothing. Not even a blip. And yet I'd still been tracking demon energy. Was there more than one demon? Possible. But how had I not felt anything when I'd been holding a demon's hand?

Bryn had sidled up next to me without my immediate notice. His eyes glowed, throwing shadows on his chiseled face. Without a word he reached for me, his fingers gliding over my scalp again. "This hurt?"

I lifted my gaze to meet his. "Not anymore."

And then his lips were pressed against mine, tongue delving in to ravage my mouth.

Surprise ricocheted through my system, quickly replaced by a tidal wave of lust pummeling into me, and sweeping through my body. Whimpering, I hooked a leg around his hip, letting him press me into the counter, his hard muscles awakening something dormant within me. I pivoted against him, luxuriating in need. A low growl rattled in his chest, vibrating against mine.

And just as quickly as the kiss had begun, it ended.

Blinking dazedly, I eyed Bryn who was now halfway across the kitchen. He ran his hands through his hair, scowling. "That shouldn't have happened."

I nodded. "You're right. But I got knocked unconscious and still have a lump on my head. What's your excuse?"

"My excuse? You kissed me!"

"I most certainly did not," I scoffed. "I was just standing there minding my own business, eating some cookies when boom," I pressed my fingers to my bottom lip, his decadent taste lingering, "you were attached to my face."

"Attached to your face? No. You were climbing me like I was a damn tree, and I reacted like any red-blooded dragon would. At least I managed to come to my senses before things got out of hand."

"That's not what happened at all!"

He quirked one dark eyebrow. "You weren't grinding against me like a cat in heat?"

My cheeks warmed. "You kissed me, and I have a head injury! I can't be held responsible for my actions until I'm fully healed." I crossed my arms over my chest, glaring at him. "We're partners, Bryn. Partners who aren't even going to be friends, according to you. So you best keep your stupid tongue, and hard body to yourself or you'll be sorry!"

My chest heaved. *Cat in heat? Seriously?* "And stop with the stupid analogies, by the way, they're super annoying!" Even though I had a tendency to use them myself. It was just ... Truthfully, everything about him in that moment was annoying. Especially how much I wanted him to kiss me again.

His lip curled into a snarl. "I already am sorry."

Okay, this is going nowhere fast. Spinning around, I grabbed another cookie, and shoved it into my mouth before I could say something I regretted. When I was finished I grabbed another, rinse and repeat, until I polished off the entire plate. Bryn remained still and silent the entire time, which made me want to scream.

I internally shook my fist in the air. *This is what you expect me to work with, Daegus? This is who I'm stuck with until my dying breath? I thought you loved me!*

"Talia, look, I—"

Raising my hand in the air, I kept my voice carefully calm, and my gaze averted. "No. Stop. I don't want to hear another apology. You are a grumpy, infuriating, delusional dragon. And those are just a few of the reasons I've decided you were right about us being friends. And what I mean is that we aren't ever going to be friends. So just leave me alone, and stay out of my way unless we're on a hunt."

"Fine," he growled. "We'll resume the hunt tomorrow after a good night's sleep." He sifted away.

My blood boiled. Even though I hated to admit it, I knew he was right about us needing a bit of rest. I couldn't stand the thought of the demon out in the world wreaking unknown havoc, but I wouldn't do anyone any good until I was fully healed and could think straight. Even still, it would be my decision, not his. "I decide when we resume the hunt! Not you! Do you hear me, Bryn O'Bannon? I decide when and where a hunt happens! The unicorn, not the dragon!"

He popped into existence directly in front of me, his expression blank. "When and where, your majesty?" He bowed deeply, peering up at me through his midnight lashes, his eyes glinting with mockery.

Your majesty? If he thought that was going to get deeper under my skin, he was wrong. Lifting my eyebrows, I delivered him an imperious look. "We'll resume the hunt tomorrow after we both get a good night's sleep."

His nostrils flared. "As you wish."

I fought the urge to roll my eyes. *Who does he think he is, Wesley from* The Princess Bride? Of course I wasn't going to complain out loud about him agreeing with me, even if he was doing it in a smartass way. "That's right, it will be exactly how I wish. Oh, and don't forget to pop over to retrieve Faith if you already haven't. I don't need any more parking tickets." Whirling around, I flung my hair over my shoulder and sashayed out of the room.

Bryn's scent lingered, surrounding me in a lust-causing cocoon. He was as sexy as he was infuriating; that one little kiss revving me up more than I'd ever been before. *I need to get out more. Mingle with other supernaturals.* Now that Daegus wasn't around, I could actually have a love life. One that didn't include Bryn … or any dragon for that matter.

First thing's first. I had to wash all remnants of Bryn from me both literally and metaphorically. Slamming my bedroom door behind me, I inhaled several deep, centering breaths. I made quick work of stripping, and beelined straight for my bathroom.

Groaning, I stopped short. Stretched and floating in my ginormous tub was a mermaid. Her ebony skin, and blue and purple tail glistened from my essential bath oils. Her wet hair was heaped on top of her head, my expensive conditioner bottle empty beside her. "Aw, come on," I muttered. "Now is not the time, Maddie."

"You said I could use it anytime you weren't, and I need to get ready for a date."

I sighed. Maddie made her home in the lake on my property. I allowed her to stay because we were friends. She thought I was fae, so I had to keep my distance to prevent her from figuring out my true nature. It was for both of our safety. Although she made it truly difficult the way she crossed boundaries. I'd never said she could use my bathroom any time without first asking, but I knew it was useless to argue with her. Mermaids were accustomed to getting their way.

"Well I'm here now, and you have an entire lake to get ready for a date in. And you can use your magic, you don't need my bath products." I snatched my empty conditioner bottle, and glared at her before dropping it dramatically into the trash.

She flipped her fin up from the water, waving it around as she regarded me quizzically. "What's got your panties in a twist?"

Nibbling my bottom lip, I considered what I could tell her. She thought I was not only fae, but royalty, hence Daegus being my bodyguard. Bryn could be explained away under the same guise. "I have a new dragon."

"Oh?" Her lavender eyes sparkled. "Is he as scrumptious as Daegus? I could use some new eye candy."

I crinkled my nose. "Ew. How many times do I have to tell you that Daegus is not scrumptious? He's like my father."

"But not mine." She winked.

"Just stop, okay? Fantasize about Daegus on your own time. We're talking about the new dragon, who, yeah, okay, is hot. If you like arrogant asshats."

Maddie smirked as she wrung her indigo hair out. "I didn't realize your type was arrogant asshat. Explains a lot."

Grabbing a towel from the closet, I wrapped it around

my middle. I wasn't comfortable chatting in the nude, unlike Maddie who thrust her pert breasts in the air as she stretched. I averted my gaze. "Arrogant asshat isn't my type. I'm just starved for romantic attention because Daegus never let me socialize with any supernatural males after the incident that shall not be named."

Maddie pulled herself up, flopping with a thud onto the floor. Slithering a few feet, she grabbed her own towel. "Well, now that—"

The bathroom door slammed open, revealing Bryn. His gaze swung around warily, landing on Maddie, and then me. "I heard a crash. What happened?"

I groaned. "You can't just come in here unannounced! What if I'd been naked?" Thank the stars I'd put the towel on when I did.

Maddie reached out one long, elegant arm from her position on the floor, not bothering to transform her tail into legs so she could stand. "Well, hello there. You must be the new dragon. Pleased to meet you."

Bryn ignored her. "Your safety comes before your modesty."

"I'm not in any danger in my own bathroom. We have so many wards on this house that—"

"I didn't know if you were fully healed yet."

I swallowed my retort. How could I fault him for being worried about me? "I'm fine, Bryn. Can I please get a little privacy?"

"Who's she?" he demanded, as if he was only just then noticing Maddie.

I heaved a sigh, sudden exhaustion weighing me down. "Never mind," I mumbled. "I'm going to bed."

Stumbling into my room, I threw myself across my bed face down, not even bothering to change into PJs and out of the towel. A moment later, my comforter settled over my back, accompanied by a swirl of Bryn's clean scent.

I listened as his footsteps retreated.

"You're going to have your hands full with that one," Maddie called from the bathroom. "Want me to sing you to sleep?"

"No," I grunted. "Just get ready for your date." *She probably just wants me to go to sleep really fast so I won't bitch about her being in my bathroom.*

Despite my protest, Maddie began humming a lilting tune, the notes haunting, and yet soothing. The magic woven into the song knocked me into instant slumber, just as she'd planned.

Chapter 6

Stretching, I yawned, blinking into the dim morning light. Several cardinals were perched on my balcony railing, their beautiful melodies weaving together to form a cheery tune. Pressed up against the glass were a few of my furry friends, waiting for me to bring them breakfast. Smiling, I dropped my towel, threw open the French doors, and plodded outside into the chilly morning. Goose bumps erupted across my flesh, but I didn't mind. My optimism had been replenished in my sleep. I was no longer angry at Bryn, but back on the 'we're going to be BFFs' train. We'd both been cranky the day before, and with time, our relationship would bloom and flourish.

Bending to scoop up the container full of nuts and seeds, I popped the lid open. "Is this what you're waiting for? Huh?" I cooed, my wildlife buddies swirling around me.

I hummed a little ditty of my own as I flung the food across the deck, watching with glee as my woodland friends happily ate. Sometimes it was the little things in life that could bring peace. I stood there a few more moments, enjoying the dawning of another beautiful Tennessee day, before dashing back inside, the cold finally causing my teeth to chatter.

"What the hell are you doing?" I snatched the discarded towel up off the floor, wrapping it around my middle as I glared at Bryn. He was leaning against my bedpost, his head tilted slightly as his gaze traveled over me with intimate hunger. "Hello?" I snapped my fingers. "What are you doing in here?"

He cleared his throat, jerking his head up. "I heard the floor creak, so I figured you were up and about. I came to find out when you wanted to head out to hunt the demon."

"And how long have you been standing there?" I internally cringed. It wasn't like I was embarrassed by nudity, I was a unicorn shifter after all, but the thought of Bryn watching me naked while I pranced around completely unaware left me feeling uncomfortable … and something else I didn't want to admit even to myself.

Bryn's gaze flitted down my body, and back up, as if he was imagining me without the towel again. My teeth stopped chattering, and all traces of goose bumps instantly disappeared as my skin heated. "Long enough to witness you out there feeding the animals while you sang and danced around," his eyes sparked with mirth, "like a damn Disney Princess."

I notched my chin up. "I'm pretty sure the inspiration for *Snow White* was my mother. Although no one knew what she truly was."

Bryn blinked. "No shit?"

I shrugged, moving towards the bathroom. "Unicorns have a way with animals."

"I could have figured that one out for myself." He nodded at the red squirrel who ran ahead of me, tail waving in the air playfully.

"I'll be down in a bit to make breakfast. I want to take a quick shower first." And I wanted some time to center myself after yet another disastrous interaction with Bryn. I'd envisioned waking him up with the aroma of a home-cooked meal. Not him finding me naked on the balcony. Things kept getting more and more awkward between us, especially after our kiss. *No. Don't think about that, or the fact he's in your room and you're only wearing a towel. You're shifters, both of you, nudity doesn't necessarily equate anything sexual for either of our species.*

Partners. Partners. You and Bryn are going to be partners, and BFFs. Nothing more. Ignore the fact that he's insanely attractive ... for a moody dragon.

"You're going to cook breakfast?" Bryn's voice went up a few octaves, causing him to sound younger than he actually was. "Wh-what are you going to make?"

I chuckled. "Whatever you want."

His eyes widened. "Really? Even blueberry pancakes?"

"Sure. But you'll have to pick up anything from the store I don't have. I—"

"Done." And poof, he was gone, sifting away before I could say another word.

Shaking my head, I scampered into the bathroom, and hopped into the shower. *Yes, Bryn is definitely run by his stomach.* I grinned evilly. *I can work with that.*

"GO SIT DOWN," I ordered, swatting the air with the spatula. "I can't concentrate with you breathing down my neck, literally."

Ignoring me, Bryn leaned in, his gaze filled with avarice. "They smell good. Did you—"

"Yes, I made them just the way you requested, extra blueberries and buttermilk."

He grabbed a plate, hovering beside me, ready to pounce.

"Bryn," I chastised. "I'll bring them to you when they're done. The first batch are throw-a-ways. You act like you're starving to death."

"Dragons need to eat a lot. Plus, it's been years since anyone's cooked for me."

"What about your parents? They didn't—"

"Can we not ruin breakfast by talking about my adoptive parents?" he grumbled, scuffling over to the kitchen table. He flopped into one of the chairs, the wood groaning in protest against his size.

"Good morning!" Maddie sing-songed as she strode in through the back door, wearing nothing but a tiny metallic bikini. Not surprising since September in the south was often still sweltering. Plus, mermaids were impervious to cold. "I smelled something delicious and decided to come check it out."

"How was your date?" I asked.

"Don't want to talk about it."

Flipping one of the pancakes, I snorted. "Seems to be a theme this morning."

"Are you always here?" Bryn grumbled, eyeing Maddie with disdain.

I rolled my eyes. "Nice to know I'm not the only one who annoys you."

"He is quite the cranky dragon," Maddie interjected. "Thought it was just Daegus, but maybe it's the entire species."

"Ha, ha," Bryn responded. "Or maybe being a warrior stuck in a house where—"

Spinning on my heel, I glared at Bryn. "You better watch it or I might decide to take away your breakfast privileges." His mouth slammed shut, and his gaze immediately skittered away. "That's what I thought."

"So, Talia, darling, remember how you mentioned last night that it was time for you to get out there and start mingling with available male supernaturals?"

"Yeah, what of it?" I scooped the first several pancakes into the garbage, and poured fresh batter into the pan, licking my finger.

"Well, guess who I heard was asking about you—"

Bryn's fist slammed against the table, several fissures creeping out from the point of impact. "No. Absolutely not. No dating."

"I can date if I want."

He shook his head. "No. I was told to not let you date —ever."

Ever? As in ... Ever? Oh, hell no. Red-hot fury burned through my system, so much that I wasn't sure what to do with it. Marching over to the corner of the kitchen I blindly grabbed at a box in my arts and crafts station. "Ever? Ever? Is that what you think? Well—" I ran at Bryn, letting the contents of my hands open over his head. A cascade of rainbow glitter fell over him, covering his head and face. He blinked up at me, sputtering. I simply stared at him, frozen in place.

Maddie's arm shot out, pointing at him as she guffawed. "You've been glittered!"

I nodded with enthusiasm. "Yeah, you've been glittered. Good luck getting all of that off of you anytime soon. You'll be finding pieces in your ears, and other," I cleared my throat, "places months from now."

Swiping at his face, Bryn glowered at me. "Mature."

I shrugged. "You don't know annoyance until you've been glittered." Not that I'd ever done it to anyone before, but glitter was the manufactured cousin of sand. Once you were contaminated, you'd never fully be free.

Dashing back over to the stove, I managed to salvage the pancakes in the pan before they burned. I sashayed to the table, dropping the stack in front of Maddie. "Bon appétit."

"Hey!" Bryn exclaimed. "I—"

"How about this—when I get to date, you get my blueberry pancakes."

Standing abruptly, Bryn narrowed his eyes at me. "Guess I'm getting pancakes somewhere else then." Without another word, he did his typical dragon disappearing act.

My stomach twisted. I hadn't meant for it to turn out that way. I was actually enjoying making breakfast for Bryn. He'd been so happy, and I couldn't help but feel— *No.* I wouldn't let another mishap with Bryn ruin another good mood. I wouldn't feel guilt for something he could have easily changed the outcome to. All he had to do was agree to my terms, and he would have been rolling in blueberry pancakes for the rest of his life. But instead he'd decided to be an asshat ... again.

Flicking off the stove, I glanced at Maddie, who was happily stuffing her face. "I'm heading up to change. Have a lot of things to do today."

She smiled around a mouthful of pancakes, and gave me a thumbs-up.

I trudged upstairs, nibbling on my lip. *I really hope things go better today with the demon than they did yesterday.*

Chapter 7

I knocked on Bryn's door, knowing he'd be in his room, basically because he had nowhere else to go. He wouldn't ditch me when there was a demon on the loose.

When he didn't answer, I toed the door, since it wasn't shut all the way. It swung open, the knob hitting the wall with a thump. "Bryn?" I called. "Where are you? We have to get a move on." My gaze swept the interior of his room, lingering on a trail of clothes leading to his bathroom, little bits of glitter attached to everything. I tilted my head, only then noticing the shower running.

"Bryn?" I called again. "Are you almost done in there?"

"Talia," Bryn growled.

I crept towards the closed bathroom door, frowning. There was no need for him to be all growly. So I'd covered him in glitter. Not mature, like he'd called me out on, but it wasn't the worst thing in the world, and he'd definitely deserved some kind of retaliation after forbidding me to date. I snorted. *As if I'm going to listen to him about that.*

A low choked rumble came from the bathroom, followed by a thump. After which Bryn said my name again. Curiosity overtook me, and I quickly turned the handle, steam billowing around me.

My gaze focused in on Bryn's silhouette outlined in the frosted glass shower door. His head was leaning against the wall, water cascading down his muscular back, as his hand … I gulped as realization sank in.

My body heated, and my pulse quadrupled in time, the scent of whatever his body wash was suddenly stifling. I fought to keep from swallowing my own tongue. *Holy shit! Bryn is totally masturbating in the shower and … and he said my name. He's taking care of himself while thinking about me!*

Gulping to return moisture to my suddenly dry throat, I froze in place. *What the hell do I do now?* The fact that Bryn hadn't heard me call out to him or enter the bathroom was a miracle in itself, one that probably wouldn't last long. And there was no way I could deal with him knowing that I saw him whacking one off, unless I wanted things to … *Nope. Not happening. Do not think about him that way. Not now. Not ever.*

Taking a tentative step backwards, I kept my gaze riveted to Bryn. *Please don't hear me. Please don't hear me.* The heel of my foot brushed up against something solid, and I swiveled to the right in an attempt to avoid whatever it was, but instead twisted my other ankle. In a ridiculous show of clumsiness, something I hadn't seemed to possess until Bryn came along, I landed in a heap on the floor.

I squeezed my eyes shut as the shower switched off abruptly. "What the—Talia? What are you doing on the bathroom floor?"

Squeezing my eyes shut tighter, I wished that said floor would open up and swallow me whole. Unicorns are mystical anomalies, with a bit of magic similar in certain ways to every species, but I'd yet to discover any power that lent itself to making me disappear in a pinch. *Can I figure out how to cast a spell to make Bryn forget only ten minutes of time? Or maybe I can—*

"Talia?" Confusion laced Bryn's tone. "What are you doing?"

"I-I was coming to see you and I heard you say—" *No! Don't say that! Don't tell him you heard him say your name!* "I … um …" Twisting around, I peeked out from under my lashes, getting one hell of a surprise. "Oh my stars! You're naked!" My eyes popped open all the way, my gaze skating down the hard planes of Bryn's sculpted body to take in every inch of him. Every single *impressive* inch of him.

He reared back as if he'd forgotten his state of undress, snatching a towel from the counter, and wrapped it around his waist.

"I have to— We need to— Hurry up and get ready so we can track the demon!" Scrambling to my feet, I dashed out of his bathroom, mortification giving me speed.

Pausing outside my bedroom, I listened intently, trepidation swirling in my gut. No sounds came from the direction I'd come from, letting me know Bryn wasn't following me. I slumped against the wall, heaving a sigh of relief. Although I knew it would be short lived.

How the hell am I going to deal with this latest development? I'd caught Bryn, my soon-to-be-BFF, going to town on himself while thinking about me. That wasn't the biggest problem in itself, nope. The real issue was ... I kind of liked it.

Swallowing, I rubbed my temples as I scrambled into my room, softly shutting the door behind me. I turned the lock a moment later for good measure. The door and the lock wouldn't keep Bryn out if he really wanted in, but it served as a mental barrier, one that I desperately needed at the moment. I knew having any kind of attraction to my guardian was a recipe for disaster, but no matter how much anyone would protest the idea, one's hormones, even a unicorn's, weren't run by the brain. *Yep, hormones are like impetuous teenagers, dead set on getting their own way despite the reasonable advice given by someone older and wiser.*

Okay. Calm down. Breathe. Just because that sexy slice of dragon has had your libido revved up since the moment you laid eyes on him doesn't mean you have to act on those feelings. It's called being mature, and having impulse control.

An image of naked Bryn danced across my brain. Groaning, I beat my fists against the wall. *No, no, no. You can't think about his sculpted abs, or the happy trail leading down to his ... NO! Think about how grumpy he is. And how much of an asshat he can be. Think about how he told you he wasn't going to ever let you date. Think about how you've known him for less than forty-eight hours and he's trying to control you. Think about his personality, and not his muscular ... his muscular anything, damnit!*

"Talia?" Bryn's deep voice rumbled from the other side of the door. "I thought you wanted to head out again after that demon?"

I cleared my throat. "Um, yes. Of course. I'll be out—" *Shit. Is my voice shrill? It definitely sounds shrill.* I needed to act normal—to get myself under control. I'd simply pretend the naked interlude in the bathroom hadn't happened. Clearing my throat again, I forced my voice back down to its normal pitch. "I'll be right out."

Sucking in a few deep breaths, I continued in my attempts to center myself. *Calm down. Nothing happened. Pretend it didn't happen. Or it was a dream. A very vivid, tantalizing dream. Shit. This isn't going to work. What the hell am I going to do?* My gaze snagged on my closet door, which I'd adorned with a *Doctor Who* T.A.R.D.I.S. decal. It was my little joke to myself that it was bigger on the inside after Daegus had remodeled it, using a bit of bartered for fae magic.

I could use a bit of The Doctor's advice at the moment. Any of them, preferably, numbers four, nine, or ten though. What would The Doctor do in this situation? Not that any of those incarnations would ever find themselves in my ridiculous predicament. No, The Doctor is brilliant, the kind of extra special I aspire to be, and yet am falling tremendously short. But still ... what would The Doctor do? He never fell victim to his hormones, or to—

Stop it. You're so easily distracted. You're like a damn dog in park full of squirrels.

If only I had some kind of catch phrase to spur me on—to center me when I was being distracted. Like Allons-y! Ugh. No. Focus, Talia. Damnit. Just focus. A catch phrase, really? Idiot. You have a demon to track, and a naked dragon to forget about ... it's not the time for frivolities.

Or maybe that was the answer after all. I had a difficult time focusing on any one thing for long periods of time. I was a unicorn with a major case of A.D.D. Or at least that's what Daegus had always said. I'd been exceedingly difficult to train when my attention flittered around to something new every five minutes. But ... but my weakness could be a strength in this situation. I simply needed something else to focus on besides Bryn. *Easy peasy. Yep. I can do this.*

Yanking the door open, I came face-to-face with ... no one. Bryn was no longer there. Guess he'd grown tired of waiting for me. *Asshat. A beautiful asshat though. No! Bryn is not beautiful or sexy, or anything but your partner. Think about something else. Anything else.*

Flicking my gaze around the hallway, my attention snagged on the bright material I was swathed in. Running my hands down my adorable retro dress, a grin slowly stretched my lips wide as I stared at the vivid pattern. I visited *Modcloth* online regularly, ordering tons of dresses for every occasion, even demon hunting. Sometimes it was difficult finding modern clothes I liked in the hues I favored. *Thank the stars for online shopping. Hmm ... I wonder if Bryn—*

"Talia?"

Squeaking, I jumped about a foot, before stumbling back into the wall. "Don't sneak up on me like that!" I clutched at my chest, my heart thrashing against my ribcage.

One dark eyebrow rose on Bryn's handsome face. "I didn't sneak. You were zoned out, standing there staring at your ... dress? What the hell were you doing?"

I blinked, dumbfounded as what to say. In the back of my mind, despite my best efforts, the scene of him looming over me naked in his bathroom was playing in a constant loop. And yet ... and yet he was such a prickly asshat. Yes, I tended to be a bit strange, and easily distracted, and ... bottom line: I wasn't perfect. But that didn't give him the right to imply I was a weirdo with the lift of an eyebrow. *I'm a unicorn, damnit! I should be treated with the utmost respect.*

My mouth opened and closed several times, anger and embarrassment warring within me. I despised feeling off kilter. My default mood was set to optimism, and yet Bryn had seriously messed with my mojo in record time.

Notching my chin up, I glared at him down my nose. "What I was doing is none of your business. It's secret unicorn stuff—stuff you wouldn't understand."

His lips twisted into a smirk. "Mmm hmm, got it. You ready to track that demon?"

Flipping my hair over my shoulder, I flounced past him. "Of course I'm ready. Allons-y!"

"What?"

"Never mind." *Add it to the list of things you don't know, asshat.*

I knew deep down that my anger at Bryn was misplaced a bit. But I also knew that anger was better than lust at the moment. I refused to let my hormones wreck our fledgling partnership. It wasn't like I could trade him in for a new dragon if things went badly.

Yep, I'll have to be the strong one for the both of us.

Unbidden, my mind conjured naked Bryn from the bathroom, and combined it with the memory of him kissing me in the kitchen. Goose bumps erupted across my skin.

Gritting my teeth together, I gave myself a mental shake, dislodging the tantalizing image. *He's an asshat, and you don't like his personality. Asshat. Asshat. Asshat.*

"I'm driving!" I called over my shoulder, hastily making my way to the garage.

Chapter 8

"Although difficult to accomplish, unicorns and dragons can be killed. I'm pretty sure a car wreck followed by a fiery explosion would do it," Bryn gritted out between clenched teeth.

"Huh. You don't say." Biting back a smile, I applied more pressure on the gas pedal.

Bryn's fingers gripped the dashboard of Faith, tiny fissures spreading out around them. *First my kitchen table, and now my ride. He needs to keep his ridiculously strong hands off my stuff.* I fought the urge to reprimand him, deciding his ashen complexion was worth a bit more damage to Faith. It amused me in some twisted way that a dragon warrior was terrified by my driving. Some would have been insulted, but not me. Nope, I chose to see the bright side of the situation. Simply by me having control of the van, I'd effortlessly made Bryn my little bitch.

Reaching for the radio, I flipped the dial on, swerving

violently to the right in the process. Nothing but static greeted me, causing me to pout. "Damn, I thought this was fixed."

Bryn grabbed my hand, and flung it back towards the steering wheel. "Eyes on the road. Keep your eyes on the damn road, Talia."

"My eyes are on the—" Heat seared the middle of my forehead, causing me to slam on the brakes reflexively. Tires squealed as we came to an abrupt stop, spinning halfway around in the middle of the street. A car honked, but I paid it no mind. "It's here. The demon is here." Without waiting for a reaction from the dragon in my passenger seat, who probably needed a change of underwear, I jumped out of Faith, leaving the door ajar.

Car honks filled the air as I sprinted down the street with a single-minded purpose. Just like before with the oddity at the park, this particular hunt wasn't going the way others normally did. Usually I tracked a demon using my magic as a beacon, the process steady as I was led to my prey. This time it was as if the demon was aware of me, and was coming to me. Not that I had a problem with it making my job easier.

"Talia! Wait!" Bryn's feet pounded the pavement behind me.

"Move Faith out of the street and meet up with me!" I commanded. It was time he learned his role in our partnership. He was my backup, which meant he sometimes had to take care of the mundane stuff when I was otherwise occupied. Daegus took over, and pushed his limits with me sometimes, but it was simply because he was like a father to me ... and Bryn most certainly wasn't. And sure, it would also be Bryn's job to make the kills, since the sight of blood made me squidgy, but only after I gave him the go ahead. *I'm in charge, damnit.*

Cutting across the street, I followed my gut, which led me into the backyard of a nearby house ...

Where a children's party was in full swing.

"Whaaa—" I muttered to myself. Purple and pink decorations hung from the deck, blowing in the warm breeze. Raucous children danced about, screaming and laughing, and amidst all of it ...

"No, no, no, no, no." I shook my head in denial, unbelieving of the horror I was being faced with. My mouth hung open, a scream building its way up my throat. I was frozen. Rooted to the ground. Of all the things I expected on a demon hunt—of all the things I was prepared for ...

A clown wasn't one of them.

The scream finally dislodged from my esophagus, escaping in a rush. All eyes were suddenly on me ... including the clown's.

"Talia?" A large, warm hand suffused heat into my shoulder as it hovered there.

I spun around, meeting Bryn's confused gaze. "Get me out of here. Now."

He glanced over my head, nostrils flaring. "The humans ..."

"Do it. Do it now. The humans will think it's a cool

magic trick for the party or something. Just—" I clutched at his shirt, tears spilling down my cheeks. "Please, Bryn."

His jaw set, he nodded once, scooping me up in his arms. "I've got you."

Blinking my bedroom into focus, I tore myself from Bryn's protective embrace, falling in a heap on my bed. I burrowed under my pillow, hoping there'd be no questions, but of course I should have known better.

The corner of the bed dipped beside my head. "You going to tell me what that was all about back there? Are you in the habit of running away from demons? Or was this one more powerful than you're used to? Come on, talk to me."

Tightening my grip on the pillow, I groaned.

"Not explaining to me what happened is unacceptable."

I attempted to burrow farther into the bed, but to no avail.

"How am I supposed to protect you, to help you, if you don't share with me what happened back there? This is why I'm here. It's my purpose to—"

Flopping onto my back, I flung the pillow across the bed. "Okay! I'll tell you. But you're not going to like it." I stared at the ceiling, unwilling to meet Bryn's eyes. "I … well, I am … What I mean to say is—I'm afraid of clowns, okay! There I've said it."

The bed began to shake, a slight tremor at first, building in intensity. Sitting up, I glared at Bryn, whose face was twisted, and mottled red, in an attempt to hold back laughter.

My lower lip trembled, and I crossed my arms over my chest. "It's not funny. I bailed, leaving a demon with a bunch of kids because I saw that clown and freaked out. I mean, I saw that thing, and all rational thought fled my mind. And what if demons everywhere figure out my weakness? Huh? What kind of demon hunter will that make me if all it takes is a clown to keep me at bay?" *And who still hires clowns for their kid's party in this day and age? I thought those creepy assholes went out of style in the 90s.*

He doubled over, clutching his stomach as the laughter escaped. "A ... clown. You freaked out ... over a human ... dressed in a clown costume ... when you hunt ... demons. Fuck." He wiped tears from the corners of his eyes. "That's priceless." Sobering, he met my gaze. "But it doesn't matter. You're not supposed to slay the demons anyhow, that's my job. You track 'em, and I end 'em. Unless it's an exorcism. So just point out the demon before running away from the clown next time."

It was true. Unicorns weren't demon slayers. It wasn't in our nature to kill or maim. In fact, we were generally passive. We weren't pushovers, but it was difficult to fight hardwired genetic traits. In olden times, centuries ago, many a unicorn had lost their lives going up against demons alone when they attempted to be both a tracker and slayer. Which was something Bryn's clan was determined to prevent with the symbiotic relationship between dragon warriors and unicorn trackers. As I stared at Bryn, determined to let his words settle me, his lips twitched ... repeatedly. He was trying, I'd give him that, although very unsuccessfully.

I shoved at his shoulder. "I said it's not funny. It's a legitimate fear."

"What are they going to do to you? Huh? I would think someone like you would love clowns."

"What's that supposed to mean? Why would you think I would love clowns?"

Bryn swept his right hand in front of him, motioning to my dress. "You love bright colors and happy things. Isn't that what a clown is essentially?"

"No! Clowns are creepy! I don't expect you to understand." I turned my head away from him.

"Fucking ... priceless," he barked out, doubling over with laughter again.

"I don't have to take this from you." Jumping off my bed, I marched over to my bathroom, slamming the door behind me.

An image of the clown from the party assaulted my brain. His bright red, curly wig flopped in clumps as he walked on his unnaturally large shoes. Lips curled back over yellow, pointy teeth, his eyes dancing with merriment as they fixated on me. Okay, so maybe his teeth weren't actually pointy in real life, but ... but ...

I shuddered, rubbing my hands up and down my arms. *Well, at least I'm not thinking about naked Bryn anymore. Bonus?* I wasn't so sure.

Sucking in several deep breaths, I mentally gathered myself. *You can do this. Ignore the clown, and ignore thoughts of naked Bryn. Just focus on the demon. There are children you need to protect at that party. Protect the children ... don't be one. Although the demon obviously would have murdered everyone at the party if that's what he was after ... clearly he's plotting something more insidious. Which is bad ... but gives me time, and assuages my guilt for running away. Okay, focus. Focus. Just Focus.*

Flinging the door open, I marched back into my bedroom, glaring at Bryn who was still perched on the edge of my bed ... laughing. "Okay, you can stop now. I'm ready to go back. I'm better than this, than my fear."

Sobering, he stood. "You sure you want to face that big, bad scary—human—very human clown?" Mirth danced in his eyes as his lips twisted up into a smirk.

"I can't decide if I should let you sift me directly back to the party, or if I should drive. Hmmm ..." Tapping my chin, I smirked right back at Bryn. If he wanted to make fun of my irrational fear, then two could play at that game.

He snorted. "The van is still parked on the side of the street back at—"

"I have a car. One that goes faster than Faith."

"You do not."

"Yes, I do." I grinned as Bryn's face visibly paled. "Well then, maybe you should apologize for laughing at me, because you know, dragons in glass houses shouldn't throw stones."

Bryn's jaw muscles popped as he ground his teeth together in annoyance. "It's completely different and you know it. My fear of your driving is reasonable, yours of clowns is ridiculous."

I lifted my eyebrows. "Ridiculous? Really? Guess I'm driving us then. But look at the bright side, with two vehicles, you can drive yourself back. So it won't be that bad."

Shaking his head, Bryn growled, "Ah, hell no." He lunged for me, snatching me up in his arms.

I beat my fists against his chest. "Bryn O'Bannon, don't you dare! I swear on everything that is Holy, if you sift me without my permission I'm going to make your life—"

The rest of my words were swallowed up into the ether as my asshat of a dragon did exactly what I'd warned him not to do.

Chapter 9

Dropping me down onto my feet, Bryn grinned as clapping broke out around us. Swiveling away from him, I bowed, the need to keep our supernatural status hidden overwhelming my anger. *But he most certainly will pay for that later.*

It only took seconds before we were swarmed by excited children, all of them smiling and tugging on our clothes while rapid-fire questions were launched.

"Shi—shizam!" *Crap.* I'd be booted from the party faster than I could say abracadabra if I swore in front of all those kids. That was the thing about demons, they liked to hide, and I had to play along with their little games as to not expose myself. In this case, I was going to have to placate everyone at the party while searching for the demon. Otherwise … well, I didn't want to deal with introducing the supernatural world to a bunch of humans, even if I somehow kept my identity as a unicorn safe. Humans knowing about demons, and dragons, would be … bad. *Understatement of the year.*

With a flourish of my hands, I yelled over the children, "I am The Amazing Talia, and this is my assistant The Brooding Bryn. And together we are Team Unicorn Talia." *Why can't I let the damn team thing go? Stupid, stupid, stupid. But too late.* I'd said what I'd said, and I was going to have to roll with it so I wouldn't get us into any trouble. The last thing I needed was for a demon to find out what a supernatural anomaly I really was. *Ever since Bryn's shown up I've been off my game. So off my game, there isn't even a word to describe how far off.*

My reluctant assistant scowled, and I winced before forcing the brightest smile I could manage. I knew what he was thinking, and I couldn't help but agree, much to my chagrin. "And we're here to amaze you with feats of magic that will … amaze you." *How many times can I say amaze in a five minute span?* It was like I had diarrhea of the mouth, and my brain had taken a sick day.

"Why are you called Team Unicorn Talia?" a chubby boy with long, dark hair asked.

I winced again before retorting, "Because our magic is unique like a unicorn's."

The little boy scratched his head. "But—"

"Just go with it kid," Bryn grumbled.

The group of rug-rats started chattering all at once, and I took the opportunity to scan the general area for the essence of the demon. Spinning in a slow circle, I came up with absolutely nothing. The demon had managed to escape me yet again. *Damnit!*

Sucking in a surprised breath, I came to a realization. The clown was gone, too. Maybe he was the demon. Could it actually be possible? "Bryn," I hissed from the side of my mouth. "The clown's gone."

He rolled his eyes. "Yeah, so? Doesn't that make you happy?" A little girl tugged on his arm, demanding his attention. He grimaced, prying her fingers away one by one as nonchalantly as he could manage.

"But the you-know-what is gone, too. What if the clown was the, well, you know?"

"Don't be ridiculous. You just want a reason to rationalize your—"

"Shut up. You don't know what you're talking about."

My gaze furtively danced over the party again, noting the gaggle of moms in the corner by the food, seemingly happy to let us entertain the children even though we were complete strangers that no one had actually hired. I was both relieved and shocked by their complacence.

"Do more tricks! Do more tricks!" A chant had begun, the volume of it growing louder and louder by the second.

My eyes widened. "Okay, um, Bryn, let's do some more magic."

"Like what?"

I shrugged. "Umm … we can …" Lunging for him, I grabbed onto his shoulders. "Get us out of here."

A moment later we appeared in my kitchen. Bryn snorted. "Well, that was brilliant."

"I'm not done yet." Scurrying for the Tupperware containers on the counter, I popped the lids open on several of them, checking out my options. About two dozen unicorn cookies were left, and I scooped all of them up, depositing them on a plate. *Did he only eat the dragon cookies? Talk about weird, and yet strangely convenient.*

Bryn leaned against the refrigerator, and crossed his arms. "Your plan is to feed the little monsters? Didn't you see the massive spread they already had at the party?"

"Go get the T-shirt I gave you."

His eyebrows lifted. "You can't mean the—"

"Yes, I mean the Team Unicorn Talia T-shirt. Don't question me, just go get it."

He disappeared, and reappeared in an instant, clutching the white cotton logo shirt in his right hand. "I don't think this is a good idea. We should just cut our losses and—"

"They've already seen us, and heard the name. We need to go with it, and what better way than to let them think we actually planned it all out," I motioned frantically to the shirt, "with merchandise to boot."

"This is going to end in an epic disaster." Despite his words, he reached for me, and the next thing I knew, we were back at the party.

"Hey!" a little girl with blonde curls shouted. "You already did that trick! Do something else!"

Kneeling down, I presented the cookies. "Yes, but did we bring you unicorn cookies and a cool T-shirt? Conjured from nowhere?"

Bryn spread the T-shirt across his chest, exposing the logo. "Tah-duh!"

"But there's only one shirt!" the same little girl shrieked. "We should all get one!"

Narrowing my eyes, I forced a smile. "Nope. That's not how it works. Only the—" *Shit.* I didn't know if the kid with a birthday was a boy or girl. Pink and purple decorations pointed at girl, but who knew? I liked to think humans were more open-minded than they used to be, even if I was usually proven wrong. "Umm ... you can only get one of these super cool shirts if it's your birthday and your amazing mom or dad hired us."

The little girl glared at me, but thankfully decided to keep her mouth shut.

"So? Come on! Who's the lucky one who gets the shirt?"

A different little girl, one with long, dark hair and chubby cheeks stepped forward, a tiny frown marring her cherub face. "But I don't like blue. Blue is for boys. Can't I get one with a pink or purple background?"

Of course. Who the hell had filled her head with such nonsense as blue is for boys? I mean, what century were we living in? *Guess humans aren't more open-minded than they used to be, or this group isn't. Ugh.* "Blue is for anyone who likes it, sweetie. Not just for boys." I twisted a piece of my aqua hair around my finger demonstratively. "I'm a girl, and I love blue. All shades of it."

"Even if that was true, pink and purple are both still better than blue."

"Now, sweetie, don't be a colorist. No color is better than any other color, it all comes down to personal preference."

"And my preference is pink or purple!" She punctuated her statement with a stamp of her foot.

"Okay, fine. Who wants a unicorn cookie?" Temporarily pacified, silence surrounded us as the children devoured our pittance of an offering.

Bryn leaned into me, and whispered, "Guess no one wants this thing. And colorist? Pretty sure that's someone who colors hair. Not what you were implying. Where do you come up with this stuff?"

"Not cool, Bryn, not co—"

"What are you?" a tiny voice rang out.

Glancing down at a frail looking boy, I schooled my expression. "We're Team Unicorn Talia, just like I said."

"No," he replied. "*What* are you? Not *who* are you?" His eyes flashed red.

Another child possessed by a demon, and I didn't sense a thing? Plus, I only came across it because I was tracking the main demon, who'd somehow managed to give me the slip ... again? What the hell?

Thinking fast, I whistled, a flurry of birds immediately responding by flocking from the nearby trees. They cluttered onto me, perching on my head, shoulders, and outstretched arms. "Don't any of you poop on me," I hissed.

The literal demon child eyed me, his curiosity waning. I knew what the birds would make him see, which is why

I'd called them. A fae. A creature most denizens of the underworld didn't care to mess with. It simply wasn't worth their time.

"Do another trick! But not with birds! They're gross!" the birthday girl trumpeted.

Turning my head, I whispered to my bird friends, "You can totally poop on her though. In fact, I encourage it. Extra points if you eat blueberries first." For the crowd, I said, "Okay, back to your woodland homes!" In a flurry of wings, they returned to where they'd come from, a few of them dropping ... gifts for the birthday girl. Unfortunately, none of them hit the target.

Bryn leaned in behind me, his breath hot on my ear. "How many tricks are we going to do? This is ridiculous."

"As many as we need to." I wanted information about the demon boy. It was too much of a coincidence that I'd tracked the demon I had a lock on twice, and twice I'd found an undetectable demon child instead. Something strange was going on and I needed to get to the bottom of it. Not to mention, I needed to expel the unwanted presence from the kid ASAP. As a general rule, demons possessing children were weak, and didn't cause much more than an annoyance for all involved. In fact, sometimes the hellish presence would be dispelled on its own as a child grew, as they garnered enough strength to take back his or her own consciousness. It was why I usually stumbled across child possessions while tracking a major baddie, and not the other way around. I could sense weak demons, but for whatever reason, they never made it onto my radar as a primary target. *But I've spotted you, you little shit, and you're getting a one-way trip back home as soon as I find out everything you know.*

Stepping in front of me, Bryn threw his arms up in the air, his fingers waving suspiciously like spirit fingers. "Well, that's it kiddos. Show's come to an end. Doing real magic wears us right out. Be sure to tell your parents about us if you want to see more."

Grabbing me, Bryn sifted.

I glared at Bryn over the counter in my kitchen, taking a swipe at him. "I wasn't done. And how the hell did you sift us into two different spots?"

"I'm not an idiot. I knew you'd be pissed, so as soon as I sifted us here, I sifted again away from you."

I tilted my head. "Really? Daegus never did that. Can all dragons—"

"I'm faster than most. There's a reason I was sent here to be your guardian. Despite what the dragon queen wanted, her order would have been petitioned against if I had grown up lacking in powers. Obviously I didn't." His arrogant expression reminded me why I'd been angry in the first place.

"Yeah, well, just because you've got dragon skills doesn't mean you get to make all the decisions. We've been over this." I motioned to myself. "Me unicorn, which means, me in charge."

"I'm not going to blindly follow orders. What were you doing back there anyhow? Huh? Or do you even know?"

"I had a plan." *Or at least the start of one.* "And even if I didn't, it's not your place to decide what happens next." Leaning over the counter, I made another grab for him, but he danced back a few steps.

"My job is to protect you, even if that means protecting you from yourself."

"Knock, knock." My back door flung open, and Maddie sashayed in. "What are you two doing?"

Bryn's eyes flashed with barely controlled rage. "Get out!"

"Don't you dare talk to my friend like that! Who died and made you King of the Asshats?"

His gaze fixated on me. "This conversation isn't over." He disappeared.

"Fine. Go hide in your room!" Slumping down in a chair, I buried my face in my hands.

Maddie patted the top of my head. "I'm getting a contact high from all of the sexual tension between you two."

"Please. So not true. He's a cantankerous asshat. Just because he's the hottest creature I've ever seen doesn't mean it makes up for his personality." I groaned. "And I'm stuck with him." I peeked out from behind my fingers. "How much did you hear?" Bryn had me more than simply off my game when I didn't immediately worry about what Maddie could have possibly heard. I needed to be more careful about throwing around the U word. *Said the girl who practically just announced herself as a unicorn at a children's party.*

"Just what was said between the lines." She pursed her

lips, and winked. "Why don't you do the sexy dragon warrior and get it over with, asshat or not. In fact, I'm willing to bet he'll be a lot friendlier if you ride him into submission."

"Not happening." Unfortunately, her words triggered the return of naked Bryn looping through my brain. I rubbed my temples.

"Then we better all batten down the hatches, things are about to get tumultuous around here."

"It's not funny, Maddie. Why are you even here?"

"Seriously, I've never seen you this cranky. You need some dragon di—"

"Nope, don't even say it. And I'm cranky because … we've already been over this. He's an asshat. Plain and simple. And I'm stuck with him."

"Mmm hmm. Well, I'm off to use your bathtub. Another date tonight."

I nodded, letting my head drop back down to the table.

Would Bryn's pessimism eventually render my optimism powerless by association?

Thumping my fist against the tabletop, I stood, the chair clattering to the ground. *No. This unicorn isn't going to let a moody dragon drag her down. We will track the demon, obliterate it, and when we're done, we'll get down to being BFFs. I'll simply overpower Bryn's asshattiness with my magical unicorn optimism. I just haven't been trying hard enough.*

Chapter 10

Bryn's warm, supple lips skimmed down my neck, scorching my skin. "Talia," he murmured. "I need you."

Arching up, I threaded my fingers through his silky locks, tugging. "I need you, too. Please, don't stop."

"As if I could."

Already naked, he divested me of the last tiny scrap of clothing keeping us apart. I spread my legs fully in invitation.

"You're so fucking beautiful. How'd I get so lucky?" His glowing azure gaze met mine as he slid lower, his inky lashes sweeping down as his focus shifted.

His tongue brushed over my aching clit, wrenching a strangled scream from my throat. "Oh, yes, yes, yes," I hissed, already half crazed.

"Talia?"

"No, you can't stop. Not now."

"Talia, you need to wake up."

Eyes fluttering open, realization kicked in as light spilled in from the hallway across my face. Bryn was hovering near the edge of my bed, arms crossed over his chest, not with his face between my legs, licking me to bliss. Mortification slowly crept over me. *Did I say anything in my sleep? Does he know?*

I pulled the covers up to my chin. "Um, hey." Glancing at the window, I noticed it was still dark out. "What time is it?"

"I couldn't sleep. We need to talk."

"Oh? About what?"

"Look." He breathed a heavy sigh. "I've only been here a few days, and I know we have some adjusting to do to each other, but I—" Running his hands through his hair, he paced to the door, and back. "I don't like us fighting like we have been. We obviously both have some preconceived ideas about how things should work in our partnership, not all of them meshing ... but we need to work all of that out." Perching on the corner of my bed, he eyed me with a whole lot of hope, and just a dash of vulnerability.

No, no, no, no. He can't act all nice now. Not when my subconscious has started throwing some seriously hot dream sex with him at me. How the hell am I supposed to—I don't know—not climb him like a cat in heat?

Misinterpreting my silence, he stood. "Okay, I get it. You don't trust me yet. And I don't blame you one little bit. But know that I'm sorry for being so ... overbearing, and as you put it, an asshat. I swear I'm going to do better. And if that's not good enough, I'll do even better. I'll keep trying until I get it right."

My heart literally skipped a beat before taking off at a gallop, which was concerning on so many levels. "How about we talk when we're both fully awake?" *And fully clothed. Seriously, the male needs to put a shirt on.* I offered him a tentative smile, praying that my hands would stay where they were … under the sheets, completely kept to myself, and not roaming the sculpted planes of Bryn's chest and body. *Good thing I can't sift, otherwise I'd already be clinging to him like a damn barnacle in the blink of an eye.*

He bit the inside of his cheek, and nodded. "Yeah, okay. But we need to talk before we start tracking the demon again."

"Mmm … yep." Forcing a yawn, I flopped onto my side, facing away from him. "I'll make breakfast. Blueberry pancakes if you turn off the light and let me go back to sleep."

I was instantly shrouded in darkness, my bedroom door clicking shut a moment later. Groaning, I pulled my pillow over my head. *Is it wrong that I kind of want to pick right up in the dream where I left off?*

HUMMING A MADE-UP TUNE, I stirred the pancake batter gently, pausing to add a few more blueberries. Bryn hadn't come out of his room yet, so I was hoping to wake him up with the scent of breakfast. I kept picturing it like he was a cartoon character, and he'd follow his nose to the kitchen, feet not even touching the ground, led by the tasty aroma of my cooking. There he'd feast on my pancakes with a smile on his face, and hearts in his eyes—for the pancakes, not me. I'd already come to terms that what I did with dream Bryn, and what happened with real-life Bryn could never be the same.

After a half dozen nocturnally invoked orgasms, I was feeling chipper, and charged to one-hundred-percent full optimist power. *Bryn and I can make this work. I just know it. All he needs is a little less moodiness, and a bit more cheer. Hmm ...*

Licking my lips, I stared at the nearly completed batter. *Maybe I could— No. That wouldn't be right. Or would it?*

Maybe all Bryn needed was a push in the right direction ... from magic. I'd worked healing and other spells into my pastries before. Why not pancakes? I'd add just a touch of optimism. He'd probably never notice. He'd simply feel a warm afterglow, almost like having a glass of wine. Sure, it would eventually go away after a few hours, but then we'd hopefully already be headed in the right direction in our partnership. He himself said he wanted to work things out between us. I'd just give us a dash of magical help.

Crouching down behind the counter, I materialized only my horn, without fully shifting. Dipping it into the pancake batter, I stirred quickly, concentrating on my intentions. *Happy Bryn. Happy Bryn. Happy Bryn.* Warmth bloomed within me, flowing out into the bowl. Satisfied, I grinned to myself, commanding my horn to disappear. I swiped at the batter on my forehead. *Oops. I always forget it has to go somewhere.*

Just as I prepared to drop the first bit of batter into the pan, Bryn lumbered into the kitchen, wearing pajama pants, and a faded T-shirt, his midnight hair adorably disheveled.

Scratching at the scruff on his jaw, his gaze zeroed in on the bowl, his nose lifting into the air. "I was starting to think I dreamt you saying that you were going to make me blueberry pancakes. I mean, didn't you have embargo between them and my stomach?"

I swallowed, returning moisture to my throat. Sleep rumpled Bryn was making me thirsty. "Nope, trade is now open for your stomach to receive my blueberry pancakes." My cheeks heated, and I turned to face the stove. *Why does it feel like I said something dirty? Get your mind out of the gutter, girl!*

Grabbing a plate from the cabinet, he paused before snagging a second. "I guess you probably might want some, too?"

I shook my head. "I'm not really in the mood for pancakes this morning so you can knock yourself out." The truth was, I didn't want to risk ingesting my own magical spell. There was no telling what it would do. Plus, the more of the magic Bryn got, the better … probably. I'd never actually spelled a dragon before. *Humans were one thing ... maybe ... No, it'll be fine.* It wasn't like it was a major spell.

"Oh? Well, you didn't have to—"

"Don't worry. There are plenty of other things for me to eat. Think of the pancakes as part of a peace offering before we talk."

"Okay. You don't have to twist my arm." Situating himself at the table, he sat ready and waiting, the maple syrup already open and beside his plate.

I chuckled as I tossed the first few pancakes into the trash, his expression filling with regret. "Don't worry, the first couple are always throw-a-ways."

"I know," he grumbled. "It just seems like a waste of perfectly good pancakes. I have room for all of them in here." He rubbed his stomach just as it growled. "See, plenty of room." He smirked.

Flipping the last pancake of the second batch onto the serving plate, I made my way over to the table. "Well, here you go." I bowed, giving him a dramatic flourish. "I hope they meet your lofty expectations."

Before I even straightened my spine, he'd drowned the stack in syrup and stuffed a ridiculous amount of food into his mouth. His eyes slid shut as he groaned.

Feeling smug, I sashayed back to the stove to make the rest.

"Talia?"

"Yes?" I flipped one of the pancakes over.

"Something's wrong with my face."

"What are you talking about?" Spinning around, I

marched over to stand directly in front of him. He was still seated at the table, his plate empty. "Well," I tipped his chin up with my finger, "what's wrong with your face?"

His lips were parted in the biggest smile I'd ever seen him give, his dimples straining in his cheeks. "There's something wrong. I can't stop—" He pressed his fingers into the corners of his mouth, tugging down. "I can't stop smiling."

I rolled my eyes. "Oh, ha, ha. Funny. You could have just told me you really liked my pancakes. You don't have to be weird—" I swallowed my words. *Oh! Maybe the magic was making him loopy. This could be fun.* "I mean, thanks, Bryn. I—"

"No!" he shouted, standing abruptly, the chair scratching against the linoleum. "Something is seriously wrong with my face." He again tugged down at his lips, panic causing his eyes to light up like flashlights. "Why can't I stop smiling? I physically can't stop."

Shiii-iiit. I nibbled on my lower lip. "Umm, well, I might have mixed a bit of magic into the pancakes."

His nostrils flared. "You mixed *what* into the pancakes?" Between his angry eyes, and his now borderline maniacal smile, I was a bit unnerved. Plus, it was all kind of my fault.

I grimaced. "I know you heard me the first time. Let's not make such a big deal out of this. The magic should wear off in a few hours, tops. In the meantime—"

"Why the hell would you mix magic into the pancakes? What exactly were you trying to do?"

Wringing my hands, I stared at the floor. "I was just trying to put you in a good mood before our talk. It wasn't supposed to do anything more than give you a bit of an afterglow, kind of like drinking a glass of wine. You know, happy Bryn, happy talk."

"Let me get this straight. After I came to you and told you I would do my best, that wasn't good enough? You had to throw some magic at me because you what? Think I'm in a bad mood all the time? Have you stopped to think all of this has been a bit jarring for me, too? Or are you only thinking about how difficult it's been for you?"

"No! I mean, yes! I mean ... you're interpreting this all wrong!"

He quirked one angry eyebrow. "Am I?"

Wow. He has amazing control of his facial muscles to be able to do that while his mouth is forced to smile. Ugh. No. Focus, Talia! Focus! "Bryn, please, just let me explain before you get mad. Or more than you already are at least."

He crossed his arms over his chest, making me feel like I was suddenly five years old again. I hung my head in shame. "I'm sorry. I was trying to help. You just seem so moody all the time. I wanted to ... to help."

"You already said that. And yeah, you certainly helped things right along, didn't you?"

"I'm sorry. What I did was wrong."

"Yeah, it was." He tapped his foot against the floor. "And?"

I peeked at him from under my lashes. It was difficult

to get a read on his emotions with his false smile. "And I won't use magic on you again without your permission."

"It's a start." He disappeared without another word.

Running over to the bottom of the stairs, I called up, "I'm sorry! Can we please still have that talk?"

Silence was my only answer.

Well, crap. None of that had gone anywhere close to my plan. Maybe I needed to do better myself. Perhaps Bryn wasn't the only one causing problems in our partnership.

Okay, fine. There are no maybes. I need to take responsibility for my own shitty behavior. He was right. I've only given it a passing thought or two how things might be difficult for him coming to live with me, but then I brushed them off. Basically, I've been selfish, just like he'd said. Crappity-crap-crap-crap.

Guess it's time for me to grovel.

Chapter 11

"What do you think I should do?" I stared into the mama opossum's eyes, her pink nose twitching. Sighing, I patted the top of her head. "Yeah, I know. You have enough things to worry about." One of the six babies on her back squeaked. "Yep, I mean you little guys. You're a handful, even if you are adorable."

Slumping into my plush couch, I grabbed a handful of chips, and stuffed them into my mouth. "What about you?" I addressed the pair of raccoons on my other side. "What do you think I should do?" The raccoon closer to me snatched the bag of chips, while the other tilted its head in confusion.

I sighed again. Of course none of them would have the answer. I needed to make things right with Bryn, but I wasn't sure what the best gesture would be. Normally I'd cook up a batch of confectionary deliciousness, but I had a feeling Bryn wouldn't be excited to eat anything I gave him for some time.

Glancing over my shoulder at the stairs, I sighed yet again. Bryn hadn't come out of his room since the breakfast incident, and I hadn't drummed up the courage to even approach his door. Tormented with guilt and shame, I knew I had to be the one to make the overture, but I still wasn't sure how to go about it. Plus, we needed to move past this silly stuff because it was getting in the way of our current demon hunt. Who knew what that slippery hell-spawn was up to? It was a given that it was certainly no good, but there are so many different levels and kinds of evil.

However, instead of doing anything productive, I'd become one with my couch, communing with the local wildlife I'd invited inside, while stuffing my face with whatever I could find in the kitchen. *I'm pathetic. When did I become so pathetic? About three days ago. That's when.*

I stared blankly at the TV, a fuzzy local news channel on the screen. I didn't actually care what I was watching, just that I had some kind—*any* kind of distraction. Not that it was working.

"... is still under investigation, but since all children were returned unharmed, even though it remains a mystery, the parents and local law enforcement are overjoyed. The biggest puzzle still remains that the children have no memory of their bus going missing or where they went ..."

My ears perked up, and I slid forward, perching my elbows on my knees. *Children on a bus going missing? What's this?* It couldn't be a coincidence. Everything inside of me was energized, tuned completely into the story. My gut churned as if I'd chugged a bottle of acid, letting me know there was a connection with my hunt and this story.

"Several parents have informed us that they will be taking their children to be analyzed by a psychologist or therapist, hoping the memories can be uncovered."

Jumping to my feet, I waved my arms around. "Bryn!" I screamed. "Bryn! You need to get down here quick! The news! You need to— Bryn!"

He appeared near the couch, causing the animals to scatter. His magically enforced smile was still present, although wilted a bit around the edges, which I took as a good sign. *He'll be back to his usual scowling self in no time.*

"What is it, Talia?"

I waved at the TV. "I just saw a news story about a bus full of kids going missing. But they were returned completely unharmed, and with no memory of where they went. It can't be—"

"A coincidence? Probably not. How long were they missing? What about the driver? Were traffic cameras checked? How about—"

"I didn't see the entire story. I just caught part of it, but I'm sure we can find all the details online."

"Hmmm," he grunted.

Tears pricked the corners of my eyes, and heat crept up over my neck and chest. I'd sworn to myself that I wouldn't do it—that I wouldn't cry in front of Bryn because of what happened. But I wanted things to be good between us. I couldn't take the tension for one second longer. "Bryn," I started, choking back a sob. "I-I didn't mean … I was trying to think of a good way to make it up to you, but I—" The tears erupted, spilling down my cheeks.

"Talia." He stepped into me, his thumbs sweeping at the trails of salt tracking down my face. "Please, don't cry." His eyes glowed, belying his emotions, despite the smile on his face.

"I didn't realize how selfish I was being. I told myself this all must be hard for you, too, but I didn't make allowances for that fact. I guess I expected you to actually want to be here … with me. I mean, we're kind of stuck with each other, but I wanted you not to feel obligated. I wanted you to be my friend." I sniffled. "I know you were uprooted from your home, twice, I guess, and your entire life has been honed for this purpose." I sniffled again. "Please know that I'll stop trying to force you to be someone you're not, because I want you to make your own choices. You've had enough taken away from you already."

He expelled a long breath, his eyes searching mine, before his gaze dipped to my mouth. "You've got crumbs," he brushed my lower lip gently, "here."

My skin tingled where he'd touched me, heating my blood. Clearing my throat, I said, "Tell me what I need to do to make things right between us."

Pulling away from me, he focused on the TV. "Guess we should do some research to uncover the whole story about the ex-missing children. Maybe we'll find a clue."

Despite everything, I couldn't help but laugh. The optimist part of me always did that ... searched for things to lighten the mood no matter the situation. "Will you say jinkies if you do?"

"You want me to say what?"

"You know ... jinkies, like Velma said in *Scooby Doo* when they found a clue."

He blinked at me. "What are you talking about?"

"You mean to tell me you never watched *Scooby Doo*?"

He quirked an eyebrow. "Can't say that I have."

"But you had to have at least heard of *Scooby Doo*, right? It's culturally significant. Even Daegus knew about it, and he's ancient."

"I didn't watch cartoons when I was a kid."

Jumping up and down, I smacked at his arm. "A-ha! I never said it was a cartoon! You really had me going there for a minute."

He shrugged. "Apparently it's easier to lie when I can't change the expression on the lower half of my face."

My stomach plummeted at the reminder. "Don't change the subject again, Bryn." Apparently he'd figured out how easily I got distracted, not that it wasn't painfully obvious. "What can I do to make things right between us?"

"How about we catch this demon, and then we can deal with everything else?"

A lump formed in my throat. "But I thought you wanted to talk right away?"

"We've wasted enough time, don't you think?"

I nibbled my thumbnail, staring at the carpet. "I guess you're right. Our personal issues come second to finding the demon. We've been slacking a bit."

"A bit?"

"Okay, if this was a test we both would have failed. I know it, and you know it. Now let's move on."

"Agreed." He strode towards the kitchen, glancing over his shoulder. "Coming? We have some research to do and a demon to track."

"Yep, be right there. I just need to let our guests back outside before they get into trouble. Unsupervised wildlife inside the house will not—" A loud crash sounded upstairs. I sighed. "End well. This will only take a minute."

Sprinting up the stairs, I steeled my determination. Bryn and I had gotten off on the wrong foot, and I'd been pushing him too hard because I thought he was being a moody asshat. Two wrongs definitely didn't make a right. And if I'd misjudged the situation, I was positive Bryn had as well. After all, he was a dragon. *Not that I'm a species-ist or anything, but hello, unicorn here.* I didn't have scientific data on the matter, but I'd be willing to put money on the fact that unicorns were more empathetic than dragons. Or at least they should be. I hadn't exactly been at my best since Bryn's arrival a few days ago.

"Eeep!" I screamed, adrenaline surging. My heart took off at a breakneck pace, threatening to escape my ribcage. At the top of the stairs, perched precariously on the railing, was a female with long, white hair, and golden glowing eyes. Despite her overall otherworldly appearance, she was dressed in jeans, a T-shirt, and boots. Somehow it seemed to fit her though.

"Shhh ... don't be scared," she stage whispered. "I don't want Bryn to hear."

"Lady, I just screamed. He probably already heard." *But then why the hell hasn't he sifted to my aid yet?*

Her lips tipped up. "Nah, I pulled you out of time for a moment."

Alarm spiked through my system. *This is not good. Whoever she is, she's damn powerful. Maybe even more powerful than me.* I needed answers. "Who the hell are you?" I demanded, hands on hips with false bravado. "And how did you get past my wards without an invitation?"

"Don't worry, I'm not here to hurt you, which is why I slid so easily past your wards. I just wanted to stop by to ... help you."

"Help me? With what, the demon?"

She laughed. "No, that's all you. I want to help with Bryn."

Confusion shot through me, replacing my fear. "Bryn? What can you help me about to do with him?"

She flipped her hair over her shoulder, her expression growing smug. "I am the reason he's here, after all."

White hair, glowing eyes ... it finally clicked. "You're the dragon queen?" I clapped, jumping up and down. "Oh! Oh! Oh! I have so many questions!"

"No time for that."

I stilled, frowning. "But you just said you pulled us out

of time, which means technically we have all the time in the world because there is no time happening around us at the moment."

She puffed out a breath. "Unicorns. You all think you're so smart, probably because you are. Fine. Whatever." She waved her hand dismissively. "Technically, we do have the time, but I came here to tell you something important, and not play twenty questions. I have other things to do today, and although I have all the time, definitely not the energy."

I rolled my eyes. "You must be so busy. You know, having time and space at your beckon call."

"I am in fact busy. You have no idea how full my plate is with all the meddling in timelines I do. It's not as simple as it seems. Plus, my *Anam Cara*, Khol, hates it. If he had it his way ..." She giggled and blushed. "Well, never mind about that part." She licked her lips. "Usually I bring him along, buuut this ... this thing with Bryn is something I had to do on my own. I'm not sure Khol would understand."

Curiouser and curiouser. "Okaaay, so spill it then if you're in such a hurry. What did you come here to tell me about Bryn that's so important?" I was pretty sure I would jump out of my skin if she didn't tell me soon.

Sliding off the railing, she stepped closer to me, her eyes glowing brighter. "He needs you, Talia. He needs your special brand of optimism. Don't give up on him. His life hasn't been as easy as you might think. It's tough being an outsider in your own clan. Especially for a half dragon."

I blinked rapidly. "What does that mean? What's his other half? Does he even know? And needs me? Hell, he doesn't even want to be my friend."

"Please, you know how some male dragons are, they have the emotional capacity of a five-year-old boy tugging a little girl's ponytail on the playground. Bryn doesn't want to be your friend because he wants more. No one told him it wasn't allowed for you to be BFFs. He's being the lovable asshat you've come to know because he likes you more than he ever has anyone before and he's your guardian. Duh. Bryn has this stupid idea about duty coming first." She rolled her eyes. "The more things change the more they stay the same." She heaved a sigh, before meeting my gaze again. "And as for the rest … It means just what it sounds like. I'm not giving you a riddle to solve. Everything else isn't my business to reveal."

No one had put the kibosh on a friendship between Bryn and me? Was he really being that guy? And why had the dragon queen taken the time to know as much as she did about Bryn? "Why do you care so much about him?"

"I put him with his adoptive parents for a reason. Everything I do is for a reason. Sometimes the only way to reach an outcome is to take a round-about route, and that was his. I needed to get him here with you, and what I did was the only way."

"But why? Why was it so important for him to be my guardian? Does it have anything to do with me at all, or is it all about him?" The more she said the less I understood.

Was she encouraging us to be friends ... or more? And what business was it of hers? Who was Bryn to her?

"Of all the beings in the universe, I wanted him here with you. No one else would do. I've gone to a lot of trouble to make this happen. So I came to ensure things stayed on course the way I planned. Like I said, meddling in timelines is tough work."

My mouth hung open, a million questions making their way from my brain to my lips, but not fast enough.

"Welp, gotta go. Remember what I said. Tah-ta, Talia." She winked, and then poof, she was gone.

The queen, too? Is there a dragon out there who doesn't pop around from here to there without warning? Well, at least she said good-bye, I supposed. That was more than—

"Talia!" Bryn called from the kitchen. "What's taking so long?"

"Be right there!"

I'd have to think more about what the dragon queen had said later. I didn't have time to decode her words at the moment. Nope, for now I had to concentrate on the demon, and smiting it off the face of the planet.

Chapter 12

Nibbling my thumbnail, I stared at the computer screen, not really seeing what was right in front of my face. My mind was elsewhere, despite the knowledge that I needed to be focusing on the task at hand. *Demon, demon, demon. You need to find information on the ex-missing children and the possible link to the demon.*

But I couldn't stop thinking about my brief meeting with the dragon queen. It had been strange on so many levels. Why was she interested in Bryn's well being? She seemed to genuinely care about him, and yet … how was that even possible? Bryn claimed they'd never met. Plus, she couldn't be much older than him. The way she dressed was a dead giveaway. Ancients, no matter how hard they tried, often clung to habits and styles from their youth. The queen felt young … relatable, like we were communicating from the same generational pool of information. So, if they were the same age, how had she sent him to his adoptive parents when he was just a baby? Unless she'd done it while still in diapers herself, which was ludicrous. I knew she had the ability 'to see' but, was she also able to time travel? She had popped us out of time, but not existing is easier than propelling oneself through time and space. At least I was pretty sure that would be the case. *Or maybe I watch way too much* Doctor Who, *and I've convinced myself I know all about time travel. Hmmm ...*

"Talia, are you paying attention at all?"

I blinked Bryn's hand into focus, which was currently waving right in front of me. "Oh, um, I was just thinking." Not a lie. I just wasn't thinking about the demon hunt.

"Anything pertinent?" he asked, skepticism lacing his tone.

I grunted, studying the cracks in the kitchen table. "You know, I've had to travel all over the world to track demons, and this one is literally right in our backyard. This whole thing has been off from the beginning. It's almost as if the demon is coming to me, instead of the other way around."

Bryn scratched his jaw, his forced smile still in place. "You've never had one this close before?"

I rolled my eyes. "Of course I have. Demons love Music City as much as the droves of humans who move there daily seem to. There's been an explosion of demon activity in Nashville in the last couple of years." I shook my head. "It used to be relatively peaceful there. Which is why Daegus decided to build us our home here in Spring Hill, Tennessee. Far enough away from the city to feel comfortable, and for both of us to have some privacy, but close enough to a major city to have all the amenities that offers. There weren't a lot of places we've been that offered up just the right balance."

Harrumphing, I tapped my chin. "There's just something different about this demon hunt. And before you say it—no, it's not because it's my first one without Daegus. This demon ... I think it can feel me, too. Which is bad. Because if it can feel me, that's going to make it wonder what I am." A chill ran up my spine. "It won't be long before it figures it out either."

Bryn's warm hand covered mine, squeezing gently. "We'll just have to find it, and wipe it off the face of this planet before it figures anything out about you."

I snorted. "Yeah, because I've been doing such a great job tracking it so far. It's one dead end after another with a spattering of demon children to keep things a tad interesting. This has been the worst," *and most boring*, "hunt ever."

"I'll keep you safe."

I opened my mouth to throw a retort at him, something about not needing to be protected, but then I met his gaze. The fierceness of it was overwhelming, causing every atom in my body to tingle with awareness. The primitive side of me was in awe of him. He was a warrior—*my warrior*—pledged to be my guardian until I drew my last breath.

My cheeks heated, and I pulled away from him. *Damn the queen for pointing out his asshatteriness is because he likes me. Now all his whiplash inducing reactions to me don't seem so odd anymore.* "I believe you—you'll keep me safe." No, I didn't need for him to protect me technically, but I wanted him to. And I would protect him as well. That's what a true partnership was about. Having each other's backs.

His chest puffed out, and he nodded once. "Good. Okay, let's get back to work." He focused on his laptop, his eyes darting back and forth as he read what was on the screen.

I took the opportunity to study him. The way my acceptance of his protection made him seem bigger somehow, stronger. As if he was manifesting his inner feelings into his physical appearance. It was a simple thing, my acceptance, but maybe it pointed to issues deeper in him ... like needing a purpose, needing to be trusted. In reality, I didn't really know Bryn at all. A few days spent together under the same roof, and a handful of conversations about his life didn't make me knowledgeable about him, not truly. I'd been trying to rush things because I'd been lonely. I was excited about the prospect of having a friend in him ... a friend that I didn't have to keep secrets from.

Slumping in my seat, I considered the situation more. Sure, I was an optimist, always had been and always would be, but ... but was I sad deep down? It did feel like I'd been struggling extra hard to call upon my default optimistic settings lately. It wasn't just because Daegus left either. I loved Daegus, but he was like a father to me, and I needed more. *Is my unicorn biological clock ticking? Not for kids yet, that would come later, but to settle down with my life mate?* I'd heard about it happening to other unicorns before. The incessant urge to find that one person who your soul recognizes as their other half. Yes, humans scoffed in this day and age about soul mates, but not me. Soul mates existed for unicorns. Our magic drew them to us … eventually. Of course we didn't have a name for the unique bond like other supernatural creatures, simply because when we linked ourselves to another, a unicorn would form the magical connection of that species. *Is … could Bryn be? No.* It was a ridiculous concept I wouldn't even let myself consider. I would know for sure by now. *Right?*

Bryn ran a hand through his hair, his smile wilting a smidgeon, drooping more on the one side than the other. It wouldn't be long until he was back to his normal scowling self. My gut twisted at the thought. I'd gone about it wrong, definitely, but my heart had been in the right place. I wanted to make Bryn happy. I wanted a permanent smile on his face, but not from magic. That had been a quick fix, and a horrible idea. I wanted to make him want to smile every time he was around me, because I made him happy.

Slumping farther in my chair, I peeked around my laptop at Bryn, attempting to be a bit more covert. It was a miracle he hadn't noticed me staring at him yet. He was the most attractive male of any species I'd ever laid eyes on. I couldn't deny it, as much as I wanted to. And yes, being close to him made my blood boil, and skin heat in a way I'd never experienced before.

If I was secretly sad in a far corner of my psyche, then it was also possible that I was pinning all of my hopes on the chance that Bryn and I would be BFFs? It could be why I was determined to force the issue. Which would also mean ... I was pinning my happiness to another being besides myself. *Totally unacceptable.*

There was nothing wrong with love of any kind, but it wasn't healthy on any level to have it be dependent. I couldn't depend on Bryn to bring me out of my emotional slump. I had to do that for myself. When anyone lets someone else hold their happiness, then it takes away their power to change things for themselves. Plus, what if something happened to Bryn one day? What if I grew to love him, and he was torn from my life ... like my parents had been? He didn't have to be my soul mate for his loss to crush me.

I swallowed around the sudden lump in my throat. I didn't even have one solid memory of my parents. Not a fuzzy image, or a general impression. All I knew of them was from pictures, and stories. So basically ... nothing. I had nothing. And yet my heart mourned their loss, or more accurately, it ached for the chance to get to know them, something that would never happen.

Sighing, I focused back on my laptop, tapping the keys to bring it out of sleep mode. I was rushing things with

Bryn. We'd eventually fall into a rhythm together. I simply had to give us both room to grow and adjust to each other. I'd been overwatering our budding plant of a relationship, causing it to drown.

"Talia!" Bryn's voice pulled me from my inner musings, causing me to jump. "Does she look familiar?" Spinning his laptop around, he pushed mine out of the way so I could see the screen.

My eyes widened. "It's the girl from the park! The one with the bodyguard who—"

"Bludgeoned you over the head. Yep. One in the same. Turns out she's the daughter of a senator."

"What? That can't be right. What was she doing at that park? I mean, sure she had bodyguards, but—"

"Yeah, it wasn't a park in the best neighborhood. Why go there even with bodyguards? But that's not the weirdest part. She went missing for twenty-four hours, and when she was found, she claimed to have no idea where she'd been or what happened. Just like—"

I slapped the tabletop. "The school bus full of kids!"

Bryn nodded. "It's all connected. All the missing people. Or I guess I should say ex-missing people."

"This is the strangest case I've ever had to deal with. Usually detective work isn't necessary." And I wasn't sure I had the knack for it. Sleuthing out answers to complicated situations was easy when there was a script, and it wasn't real life. Unfortunately for us, no one was going to clue us in before the next episode.

His eyes glinted with mirth. "Lucky me, I get the complicated case first one out of the gate."

I snorted. "You do seem to have bad timing. Or ..." My chest tightened, and my gut churned as the thought took shape. "Or someone sold me out."

Understanding washed across Bryn's features, pinching them. "You can't actually think one of my clan sold you out to a demon. If that was the case then it would have come directly for you."

"Maybe they're smarter than that. Nothing personal, but if I still had Daegus with me, him being a seasoned warrior, he would probably—"

"Do a better job. Yeah, I get it." His lips twisted down, finally able to make his signature broody pout. He fingered his mouth, heaving a sigh of relief.

"It's not that Daegus would necessarily be any better at figuring out what's going on. It's just that it would make sense for whoever to think he would be. Even if you were friggin' Sherlock Holmes, we're still in a transitional period. And if someone filled the demon in on the changing of guardians, then it would know that some of its antics might fall through the cracks until it was too late."

"Are you seriously entertaining the thought that one of my clan sold you out?" Bryn studied me, his expression indifferent.

"I don't know. The timing of it—all of it, is strange. I don't want to believe it either, but I'm not ruling it out. We can't until we're absolutely sure." Slamming my laptop shut, I stood. "But before we go pointing fingers at anyone, we need to get our hands on one of these kids."

"I'm not sure I like the sound of that."

I patted his shoulder. "Don't worry, we can lure one of them away to get some information. Then once we get it, I can easily cleanse him or her of their pesky little possession."

"Lure? Yeah, like you meant borrow?"

Grinding my teeth together, I glared down at him. "I meant to return the car, but that was before I got hit over the head by an overzealous bodyguard. If you were so worried about the morality of it then you should have popped back over there and returned it yourself. It would have taken you like what, five minutes? Me, on the other hand—"

"I knew it. You're going to kidnap one of those demon kids." He dropped his face into his hands. "I can't sift us out of jail you know. It would expose us to the humans, not to mention—"

"I'm not kidnapping anyone. I said lure, and I meant it." Spinning around, I rummaged through the junk drawer. "Now, where's the duct tape? I know I had a roll in here somewhere."

Pressing close behind me, he rumbled in my ear. "And what exactly are you planning to do with duct tape? Fix your van with it?"

I froze, a shiver running up my spine from his proximity. *How am I supposed to resist him when he keeps invading my personal space?* "None of your business," I mumbled, while covertly inhaling his tantalizing aroma. *Mmmm ...* It was a clean scent, hard to pinpoint what it reminded me of besides Bryn. It was unique to him, and already one of my favorites, even better than freshly picked daisies, or a batch of sugar cookies, or ... *Ugh. Stop. Stop thinking about his ridiculously addictive scent. But seriously, someone should bottle and sell — No. Enough.*

Shoving away from the counter, I bumped his front with my butt. *Yep, that's a good idea if you don't want to think about him naked and on top of you.* He sifted across the room, but not before I felt a not so little surprise in his pants. Mr. O'Bannon was struggling with our mutual attraction just as much as I was, which only made things worse. *I'm a pathetic, hormone-addled unicorn, he needs to be stronger than me, damnit!*

Clearing my throat, I ignored the elephant in the room by not letting my gaze drop below his belt. Despite my efforts, sexual tension still sizzled between us. "You got an address for the senator's kid?"

"Oh, fuck. We really are going to end up in jail."

Well, that was one way to kill the mood. And to seal the deal ... "Oh, and I'm driving again." Snagging the keys off the peg by the door, I strode out into the garage, knowing Bryn was hot on my heels.

Chapter 13

"Tell me the truth. This is all an elaborate prank."

Glancing at Bryn, I scrunched up my nose. "What are you talking about?"

"This," he waved his hand at me as I sped down the highway, "your driving. The demon kids. Even the magic in the pancakes. All of it since I got here. It's a prank, right? Break in the new dragon? Ha, ha! Funny. You got me. Now, please slow the hell down!"

I rolled my eyes. "You wish it was a prank."

"Yeah, I do. Did you not get that?" He grabbed my right leg, and lifted in an attempt to slow us down.

I swerved to left, almost hitting the median. "Hey! Hands off!" In retaliation I pressed down harder on the gas pedal.

"Please, Talia, I'm begging you. Slow down before you get us both killed."

Wasn't I supposed to be making more of an effort? After all, we'd agreed to have a talk to sort things out. Me antagonizing him was ... fun, but wrong. Even if it was better than the alternative: me rubbing against him like a cat in heat like Bryn claimed I did before. Sighing, I eased off the gas.

"Thank you. Now, how about you pull over and we can switch? Huh? Please let me drive."

I glanced over at him. His eyes were pleading, and combined with the ashen shade of his complexion, he was all kinds of pathetic.

I sighed again, demonstratively, throwing in a bit of an eye roll. Ever since the dragon queen put things into perspective for me about his moodiness, I couldn't seem to resist letting him have his way a bit more often. He was like an abused animal I wanted to fix one act of kindness at a time. "Fine. In the spirit of making things good between us, I'll let you drive."

"Thank fucking god."

I bit my tongue, swallowing back my retort as I slammed on the brakes, sliding to a stop on the shoulder of the road. Before I could even unbuckle my seat belt, Bryn was out of Faith, and yanking the driver side door open.

Gripping the steering wheel, I ground my teeth together. "Don't be so eager about it or I'll change my mind." Even I had my limits.

He lifted one eyebrow. "So you want me to lie to you?"

"No," I grumbled. But damn, I was going to shave off

his eyebrows one day. They were always waggling all over the place being too expressive, and just plain judgmental.

A four-wheeler truck zoomed by, shaking Faith, and blowing my hair into my face. Bryn's long fingers glided behind my left ear, tucking the thick strands back. Our gazes clashed, sizzling with the sexual tension I just couldn't seem to avoid no matter what situation we were in.

"You just going to stare at me all day or are you going to move over?" His voice was rough and low, an intimate caress along my senses.

"Um, yep … moving now." I awkwardly pushed myself cross the cracked leather, and then scrambled over into the passenger seat.

Bryn climbed in, and started fidgeting with the seat. "How can you drive like this? It's a driver's seat, not a lounge."

"I don't like to have the steering wheel touching my chest, like some people." As if to prove my point, he yanked the lever, causing the seat to pop forward.

"What worries me is whether or not you can see over the steering wheel when you're driving."

I crossed my arms over my chest. "I can see just fine. Are we going to go, or what? Or would you rather sit on the side of the road all day? Or—" My eyes widened. "You're stalling, aren't you?"

"Don't be ridiculous." He adjusted the rearview mirror, glancing in it several times.

Smacking at his arm, I growled, "You are! You're stalling!"

"Fine! I am!" He ground his teeth together, and smacked the dashboard. "Can you blame me? I'm not a fan of the possibility of jail time."

There I was making a consorted effort to wave the white flag, and he was trying to throw a wrench in my plan. White-hot fury shot through my veins, boiling my blood. "Out! Get out now!" I shoved at him, and he spilled onto the pavement in a heap, Faith's door under him.

"Ow! You broke your precious van. Was that necessary?"

Before he could stand, I dove into the driver's seat, and door or not, smashed my foot on the accelerator. In a flurry of gravel, I shot forward. "Don't follow me!" I screamed. "I don't need or want your help!" *Asshat! Asshat! Asshat!* Why did I think he would be anything but an asshat just because I knew his true motivations and was attempting to make peace? *Asshat! Asshat! Asshat!*

"Hi, dragon here. I can sift," Bryn said from the passenger seat.

Swerving to the right, I slammed on the brakes, skidding to a stop. Several horns honked. "I said to get out!" Shoving at him again, my hands passed right through him as he sifted out, and then right back in.

"I can do this all day."

"Why? Why? Why?" I pummeled the steering wheel with my fists, silently cursing the dragon queen for sending Bryn to me. I wanted to fix things between us, but how was that possible when he drove me absolutely insane?

"Talia, I just don't think kidnapping the senator's kid is a solid plan. I told you before, it's my duty to protect you, even if it's from yourself."

Leaning back, I tilted my head towards the ceiling. "Doesn't matter what you think. Your job is to—"

"A partner." He cupped my cheek, gently forcing my gaze to his. "Isn't that what you keep telling me. That you want us to be partners and BFFs?"

Damn him for using my own words against me. I nodded reluctantly, not wanting to dignify him being right with a verbal response.

"If that's what you really want, you can't order me around. You can't have it both ways, Talia. Life doesn't work that way."

My lower lip jutted out against my will. "Maybe it does in my world," I muttered.

His thumb swept across my cheek. "Make up your mind what you want. Decide if you want a partner, or a mindless sword at your back."

Hadn't he told me he wasn't going to be my friend at all, let alone my BFF? When had that changed? He didn't know what the dragon queen had revealed to me. Sure, I was convinced I'd eventually wear him down, but he hadn't even put up a fight, not really. *This dumbass dragon is determined to give me emotional whiplash.*

"You know what I want," tumbled from my lips, ripe

with meaning. Cringing, I wished I could hit rewind and swallow my own damn tongue.

Bryn stared at me, his pupils dilating before the blue in his irises lit up. Several cars zoomed by, shaking Faith, but it didn't matter because I couldn't look away. I'd opened Pandora's box, and I wasn't going to miss what I'd unleashed.

He leaned closer. "Tell me what you want. Tell me exactly what you want."

I bit my lower lip, indecision causing my gut to churn. *This is such a bad idea. I can't actually tell him what I'm thinking, what I've been thinking about him.* We were attracted to each other, there were no doubts there. But creatures who lived as long as dragons and unicorns knew attraction wasn't enough for anything long term. If Bryn wasn't my personal guardian, I would have already pursued him with abandon. What would happen if I let things progress between Bryn and me, only to later have our physical relationship fizzle out? What would it be like to be stuck with an ex-lover, forced to work with them, live with them, until my last dying breath? There was more to consider than my fears of losing him if I became too attached ... What if I didn't lose him—and I wanted to? No matter how hard I tried, my optimism stayed buried on the subject of a romantic relationship between Bryn and me. *Is that my gut telling me something?* BFFs is one thing, but more? I had doubts. So many doubts.

Bryn leaned even closer, his clean scent and mint

flavored breath swirling around me. "Tell me what you want."

"I-I ..." *I want you! Naked on top of me, and under me, and behind me, and—No! Stop! Just stop!* "I don't know." It was too big of a decision to make on the side of the road in the middle of a demon hunt. I needed time, space, and a metric ton of chocolate to make sense of things.

Disappointment rolled across his features, like rain clouds settling in. He pursed his lips, settling back into his seat. "Let me know when you figure it out."

Great, it's all on me. Why? Why do I have to make the decision and the move? I'm seriously finding a new appreciation for those alpha male types in romance novels who know what you want, and press the issue, even if you put up a weak, pretend fight. Bryn needs to take notes. If he pushed, just a little — Wait. No. That's not what you want at all. What are you even thinking? Flustered, I blurted out, "So now what?"

"You're asking my opinion? Huh. I figured you would have continued on your way to the senator's."

"Mmm ... well," I twirled a piece of hair around my finger, "I suppose finding another way to talk to the senator's daughter without—"

"Kidnapping her?"

"I was going to lure her. Lure, say it with me."

Drumming his fingers against his jean-clad thigh, he chuckled. "Wasn't aware lure can be found in the dictionary as another word for kidnap. I learn something new every day."

"Ha, ha. Very funny. I suppose you have a better plan? One we can implement immediately? Because we've wasted enough time on this particular hunt. The demon should have been nothing but a memory days ago."

Scratching the scruff on his chin, a smile crept across his face. "As a matter of fact, I do have an absolutely brilliant plan."

"THIS IS NEVER GOING TO WORK," I muttered, fidgeting with the tight black blazer. I couldn't remember the last time I'd worn black, let alone all black. Top it off with my magically glamoured dark brown hair, and … booorring. The longer I was in the dowdy attire, the closer I came to depression, my unicorn soul crying out for colors, any or all of them.

Bryn stood beside me on the right, dressed in similar attire—black dress pants, and a charcoal blazer, what was commonly referred to as business casual. Of course he was decidedly more stunning than boring. I suspected he'd be delectable in a garbage bag.

"Just stick to the plan, and remember, if things go south, you've got a sifting dragon up your sleeve."

"I also have all the powers of a unicorn on my side." If only I had the ability to sift, it would make my life abundantly easier. Sighing, I reached for the doorbell. "Don't you think it's weird that they let us onto the property without an appointment?" I whispered under my breath.

"Maybe. Or maybe with the pro-violence bodyguards they have on staff, they aren't concerned about a psychologist and her assistant."

I opened my mouth to respond just as the front door swung open. Instead of a bodyguard, or even a maid or butler, the little girl from the park stood there, completely alone.

"Hello." She waved, grinning up at me. "I remember you. You were at the park." She scrunched up her nose. "I liked your hair better before." She frowned at her own hair, the ends curled into perfect blonde spirals.

Glancing over at Bryn, I shrugged. "I can only get away with unnatural shades of hair color when I'm not working."

The little girl tittered. "Please. You can stop with the pretense. Lori's parents are ... busy at the moment. I don't know exactly what you are, but I know neither of you are human ... or psychologists."

Was she referring to herself in the third person, or was the demon fully in control? Since I still couldn't sense anything unusual, I wasn't sure how her brand of demon worked. "Only I'm a psychologist, he's my assistant."

Her eyes flashed red. "I said to stop. There really is no point."

Bryn reached for me, his intent obvious. "No, don't." I stepped away from him. "Maybe—maybe we can get some information."

He ground his teeth together, but remained silent. He knew I was right. We weren't necessarily in any immediate danger, and with the little girl being so open about things, maybe she'd spill the beans about what was going on with all the possessed children.

"Okay, fine. We're not human. We came here because we're curious about what you are, and why you're here."

"If you're not human then what are you?"

I nodded in Bryn's direction. "Dragon." I pointed to myself. "Fae."

"Fae. Huh? Seelie or Unseelie? A mix of the two? I'm not really getting a sense from you. Either you're extremely powerful and are hiding it, or are too weak for me to get a read at all."

I narrowed my eyes. "Maybe I'll tell you more if you tell us what we want to know first."

She sighed. "I suppose it wouldn't hurt anything. After all, what's one little fae and a dragon going to do to all of us?"

About twenty kids, all with red eyes, stepped up behind her, peering at us with curiosity.

I internally sighed. I wanted information, but if they were going to gang up on me, I'd simply have to find the big baddie the old-fashioned way. No sleuthing necessary. I couldn't have gangs of demon children roaming around on my watch.

Shuffling back a few steps, I drew on sparks of light within me, thrusting magic out of my palms as I lunged forward, sprinkling glittering dust in a wide arc over the kids' heads. *Take that, mini-demons! Bye-bye now.* With a smug smile, I leaned against the doorframe, waiting.

Several seconds went by, and I blinked, still waiting. *It should have worked by now. Why is—why is absolutely nothing happening?*

All their little faces continued to peer up at me, red eyes focused on my every move.

Okay, maybe they're a touch stronger than I thought. Shaking my hands out, I called forth more magic, drawing it from deep in my gut. Light burst from my palms, exploding once more in a glittering dust as it rained down over the tiny demons. I grinned. *That should do it.*

The senator's daughter coughed, wiping away dust from her face. "I'm confused. Was that supposed to do something to us?" Some of the other children tittered, as if I was one big joke.

Oh, shit! My magic didn't work! If my magic doesn't work then— Abort! Abort! Abort! I reached for Bryn at the same time he came for me. He sifted us away as soon as his skin made contact with mine.

Back in my living room, I stared up at him. "That was closer than I would like to admit. My magic has never not worked on demons like that before. I—we might be in over our heads."

He snorted. "You think?"

I shoved at him. "Shut up. I need to think. We obviously need a new plan." But what kind of plan could I come up with when my magic was on the fritz? I couldn't have Bryn behead a bunch of human children to oust the demons.

Think, think, think. I need to think.

Storming into the kitchen, I located my stash of chocolate, and began stuffing my face.

I will figure this out. The demons, Bryn ... all of it.

Chapter 14

About a half pound of chocolate deep, something occurred to me: The dragon queen wouldn't have put a profound amount of effort into bringing Bryn to me, if she'd foreseen that he'd be injured or killed on the job after only a few days. I had to also assume that umbrella of knowledge lent itself to my safety. But then again, all the sugar I'd consumed could have gotten me high, causing me to be a bit loopy. Wouldn't be the first time. Despite that very distinct possibility I came to a decision.

"Bryn!" I rushed into the living room, half of a candy bar melting in my hand. "Take us back right now!"

He pushed his laptop to the side of the couch, and stood. "What? You saw all those demon kids, you can't face them when your magic isn't w—"

"The dragon queen wouldn't have sent you here just to get you killed right away."

He rocked back on his heels in surprise. "Just for argument's sake, say that part is true, what about you?"

"I'm sure she wouldn't send you here to deal with emotional trauma, you know if you let something happen to me right away. I don't think she's trying to torture you."

"Why do you think she has the ability to see these types of things at all? Not much is known about the extent of her powers. What if she can only—"

"I know I'm not wrong, Bryn. Please, just trust me."

He stalked over to me, his brow furrowed. "I'm your guardian. It's not about trust. I have to protect you. It's like a compulsion. It's in my blood to ... protect."

Inching closer to him, I scanned his face, searching for answers. "You don't just mean your dragon blood, do you?"

"No. I don't." Turning abruptly, he strode a few steps away, his head hanging low. "The other half of me isn't quite human either. My father was a guardian who hooked up with a dragon. I don't know all of the details or even how I came to be exactly, but I do know that I'm half guardian and half dragon."

"Guardian? What—well, what is that?" I set the candy bar on top of the coffee table, and licked my fingers. It would be rude to munch away on chocolate during a serious conversation ... unfortunately.

"From what I understand, there are a race of people who protect this dimension from invaders from other worlds. There are seers, who have premonitions about the potential threats, gatekeepers, who can open and shut the gates between dimensions, speakers, who can speak any language of any origin, and guardians, whose job is to protect the seers."

"And your genetic father was a guardian."

He nodded once sharply, running his hands through his hair. "Yeah, but I never met him, or my birth mother for that matter either. She was obviously a black dragon."

"Hmm ..." The more answers I got about Bryn, the more questions arose. Even his origins were strange. It wasn't like female dragons to have one-night stands, especially with a male from another species. Dragons craved finding their *Anam Cara*, and once they found them, it was nearly impossible to stray because of the magical bond.

Bryn whipped around, his eyes glowing, and his countenance fierce. "So you see, it's more than just the dragon oath to protect you that drives me, it's my guardian blood." He sifted right in front of me, leaning down. "I need to keep you safe, and your asinine plans aren't making things easy for me."

"Bryn," I touched his chest, "this job comes with risks. They're unavoidable. Plus, I'm really hard to kill."

His chest heaved under my fingers, his heart picking up speed. "I know that intellectually, but when I look at you I see this fragile creature, one that I would lay down my life to protect."

Normally being called fragile would piss me off, but not this time, not coming from Bryn. The words might not have been right, but I understood what he meant.

Plus, all creatures great and small are fragile on the inside. The survivors simply had better armor. "I thought you didn't like being sent here without a choice. I thought—"

"The moment I laid eyes on you, I knew I could never walk away, and I hated it. I hated that everything in me was compelled to do exactly what was already planned out for me. I wish it could have been my choice. I wish I came to you on my own. But I've come to terms with it. How I got here doesn't matter, just that I am. Here. With you. And I'm sorry. I'm sorry I've been ... well, the way I've been. It was all to push you away, because I wanted to be near you so much."

I nibbled my bottom lip, my heart plummeting into my stomach. I'd seen this before. Bryn was drawn to me because of what I was, not because he felt some kind of instant soul mate connection, no matter how much I wished he had. I'd even been hoping for the normal draw of lust. At least lust could grow to something more in time if given the chance. What he was talking about was blind devotion, something that was almost a compulsion. *But isn't this what you wanted? You can't be with him. This makes it easier.*

"Bryn, it's because I'm a unicorn. We have a kind of charisma, especially for supernatural beings. I'm sure you were taught about it, right? It'll make you feel things for me that you wouldn't otherwise." How had I forgotten? *Maybe because you wanted to?*

He chuckled. "Of course I know about it." He grabbed the neck of his shirt, tugging it over his head.

Stumbling back, I gasped. There on his right pectoral was a glyph etched into his skin. I immediately recognized the symbol, it was for protection ... against me, against my magic. I hadn't been aware that Bryn's clan knew of the glyph, the knowledge of it something I thought was better left lost in case it fell into the wrong hands. *Obviously they kept that one close to the vest.* "I didn't notice that before, um, when I saw you naked." I bit my thumb hard, hoping the slight pain would keep the actual image of his naked body from looping through my brain again.

He snorted. "Yeah, well, after the pancake incident, I visited Daegus. He has one just like it. Took me to the dragon who did his."

My mouth fell open. "What? Daegus has one? Wait! You know where Daegus is? He didn't even leave me a phone number. Tell him to call me!" I shook my fist in the air, as if he could hear me somehow. "And when did you go? Huh? When did you have the time?" Maybe he hadn't been sulking in his room after all. What the hell? I'd been riddled with guilt, and he'd been sifting off to who knows where?

"You're missing the point, Talia." Bryn's deep voice brought me back to the present. "None of your magic can affect me anymore, so I'm not compelled by your unicorn charisma to feel things for you." He thumped a fist against his chest. "It's all me. And nothing's changed since I got this." His fingers danced over the glyph. "It's been me from the beginning. What I feel for you is real. A part of me pushed you away for that reason, too. Before the protective tattoo, I wasn't sure I could trust my own mind or body. But now ..."

"Oh." I blinked rapidly. *At least now I understand why he did a one-eighty when it came to me.* Didn't mean I wasn't having a difficult time processing everything though. *Isn't this the exact opposite of what you want? Or is it?* I didn't have a clue anymore. I just wanted things to be simple again. Ever since Bryn blew into my world, he'd turned it upside down, confusing me like never before.

"What do you feel for me exactly?" Slapping my hand over my mouth, my face heated. While my mind had been having a data overload, the words had simply slipped out.

Cupping my cheeks in his large hands, he brushed his lips against mine. "I want you, Talia. I want to be your partner, your BFF, and anything else you're willing to give me. For the first time in my life I feel like I actually belong somewhere ... here, with you."

"But you haven't been ... I don't ... I'm so confused." I didn't know what to say or do. I was frozen with uncertainty. This moment with Bryn had come out of left field. *Unless he's my soul— No. He's definitely not. I would know. I would definitely know.*

"You're right. Words are just words, and they have a way of muddling the truth. Maybe this will help clear things up."

He savagely took my mouth, plunging his tongue past my lips. A low growl rumbled in the back of his throat as he grabbed my hair, and tilted my head at a better angle for him. I responded instantly, my mind overrun with lust.

But before I could really sink into the kiss, he pulled back, his glowing gaze searching mine.

Dumbfounded, I blinked up at him, my arms hanging limply at my sides. "But you've only known me for a few days." And that kiss spoke of yearning and desire, but for more than just the physical. It was a plea for a chance at something real. He'd been wrong, it didn't clear anything up. In fact, it had done the opposite.

He huffed out a breath, frustration causing lines to mar his brow. "Why are you so hung up on time? On how long I've known you? Does no one believe in fated connections anymore? Or love at first sight? You as a supernatural creature, a unicorn no less, should know better. I thought you were an optimist."

"Being an optimist doesn't make me gullible. Some things simply aren't real. And love at first sight is one of them." I was one of those girls who rolled my eyes at insta-love in books and movies, and yet … and yet … *Ugh. Unicorns do have soul mates. But I would know already if Bryn was mine. Right?*

Bryn smirked. "I don't love you, Talia. That's not what I'm saying. Even though I do believe love at first sight is possible. I am a dragon after all, and I've seen it with *Anam Caras.*"

More like lust at first sight. Love took time to develop, no matter what anyone said. Even with dragons who were *Anam Caras.* Plus, not all *Anam Caras* were love pairings. Some matches between dragons were drenched in brutality, the male of the species having a leg up on the female because of old magic. Even soul mate bonds with unicorns took time to build the actual relationship beyond the initial connection.

"Oh, good," I deadpanned. "It's good that you're not proclaiming your undying love for me after two days." Or was it three now? Four? My left eyelid twitched. "So what are you saying then?"

"I'm saying that I like you, really like you, despite all your ... oddities. And I want to get to know you without any of the walls we've both put up. I want the chance for something to develop, because—" He yanked me against his chest. "I've never been in love before, but I think, one day, I could see myself loving you."

I scrunched my nose up as I peered into his lipid pools of blue. "How does anyone see themselves maybe falling for someone in the future? How can you—"

"Oh, for fuck's sake. Would you just shut up already? You're overthinking this." His lips came crashing down on mine, stealing my breath, and my words.

Common sense came back to me slowly, right about the time I realized I was on the couch, Bryn's hard body covering mine, and my legs were wrapped around his waist. It was like I'd had some kind of sexual blackout the moment his lips connected with mine.

Beating my fists against his chest, I tore my mouth from his, hissing out, "Stop! No. We can't—"

He blazed a scorching trail of kisses down my neck, eliciting a wonton moan. But I would not be deterred. "I said no!" Shoving at him, he fell in heap on his ass, bewilderment causing him to scowl.

"Okay. I heard you. No. Even us dragons have been taught a thing or two about consent. I won't touch you again ... unless you beg for it." Standing, he slid his hand down the front of his pants, adjusting his erection.

I ground my teeth together as I straightened my dress. "Unicorns don't beg." *What is happening here?* How had things gotten out of hand so abruptly? Bryn fought even being my friend, and then all of a sudden he wanted some kind of romantic relationship. I gulped. That thought absolutely terrified me. I narrowed my eyes at him. Was he tricky enough to do reverse psychology on me? Had he realized he wasn't strong enough to resist the pull we had for each other, so he'd flipped the tables, putting it all on me? Could he think by pushing me for something more that I'd run away scared? Maybe he simply wanted sex, which I couldn't blame him, we'd be amazing together—

I shook my head. *No. stop. Demons. No time for personal drama when there are a bunch of demons on the loose. Demons who aren't responding to your magic.*

"Bryn, you need to sift me back to the senator's house. All of these ... distractions can wait until after the hunt is over."

His jaw went slack. "You did not just call me, and what was happening between us, a distraction." Shaking his head, he strode into the kitchen. "Fuck if I don't feel like a chick right now."

Suppressing laughter, I scurried after him. Bryn was

one of a kind, that was for sure. *I suppose I like his oddities, too. Life will never be dull with him.*

I halted abruptly. *Shitty, shit, shit.* Beyond lust, I could completely see myself falling for Bryn. In that moment, I came to understand exactly what he'd been babbling about. It was possible to know that it would be easy to fall for someone. *Does that mean I'm already falling? And if I am, could that point at something more? Like maybe he could actually be my soul mate?*

Standing there, staring after my asshat of a dragon, I felt like I was on the precipice of something. Like I was poised for an unknown adventure, a free fall into terror or bliss ...

And all after just a few days.

I'm so screwed. Soul mate or not.

Chapter 15

"If you don't take me back there then I'm just going to drive myself." Placing my hands firmly on my hips, I resisted the urge to smack Bryn. Despite our moment in the living room minutes earlier, when his lips had set my entire body on fire, I still wanted to strangle him for his controlling asshattery ways. *Is this how it's always going to be?* I wasn't sure I could handle the turmoil on a long-term basis.

"I'll simply sift you back. Have you forgotten about your magic not doing a damn thing to those little red-eyed punks? Nope. You're not going anywhere I don't want you to." He smirked, obviously high on his power trip.

"This isn't a partnership either," I hissed. "This is you thinking you can control me." My anger won out, and my hand connected with his chiseled jaw. He didn't even flinch. "I won't have you dictate what I can or cannot do, even if you're doing it under the guise of protecting me."

He growled low in his chest, as if the dragon in him was threatening to break free. "It's not a guise, Talia. It's a dumbass move to go into a den of demons on a hunch when you have no defenses against them at the moment."

"So, what do you propose we do then? Huh? All we've been doing is a big bunch of nothing since the start of this hunt." I stamped my foot. "This is not how any of this is supposed to go. I need to get answers so I can put an end to whatever is going on with this demon infestation in Tennessee."

"We'll think of something, just give it some time. Maybe your magic needs recharged or something. Whatever it is, we'll figure it out."

Frustrated, I darted past him, dashing for the garage. I snagged the keys to my spare car, silently cursing Faith's temporary out of commission status. My second car did not go faster than Faith. In fact, I'd be lucky if it started. It was nothing more than an old, rusted hunk of junk that I didn't even know what make or model it was. *Stupid Bryn for making me resort to this.*

"Really? Obviously you didn't hear a word I said in there." Bryn hooked his thumb in the direction of the kitchen. "I'm not letting you go."

"You can't stop me," I gritted out.

"Watch me." He leaned on my car, and crossed his arms.

"Get out of the way, Bryn. I mean it. I don't want to have to hurt you."

His gaze slid up and down my body, the corners of his eyes crinkling as he choked back a laugh. "As if you could. I'm a dragon, a warrior, trained in combat since I could walk, remember?"

"Yeah, well I'm a unicorn trained in combat. Who do you think would win, a dragon or unicorn?"

"Always a dragon," he scoffed, rolling his eyes. "Daegus probably didn't go that hard on you. He was probably afraid he'd break you. It's not in a unicorn's nature to be a warrior. You can't even stand the sight of blood."

Oh, no he didn't. Unlike his comment about being fragile from before, this time he'd straight up insulted me. *I'll show you breakable.* And fine, so unicorns weren't generally warriors, but that didn't mean I couldn't kick ass when I needed to.

Shifting just my horn into existence, I lowered my head and charged. A buzzing sound had taken up residence in my ears, and I could see his mouth moving, but the words were lost to me.

He sifted before I ran him through, reappearing directly behind me, grabbing my horn. "Are you actually trying to stab me with your horn?"

"I would have healed you, after you suffered a bit." The truth was, I wouldn't have been able to do it. I'd let him stop me. Which pissed me off even more because it meant he'd been right about me. Shifting my horn away, I spun, barreling at him with both fists raised. He grabbed my wrists, smashing me into his chest.

"Stop, Talia, this is pointless."

Shrieking, I struggled to pull free, only ending up restrained more tightly against him. Sadly, even though my mind was immersed in scenes of violence, my body had other ideas.

Before I realized what I was doing, I was up on my tiptoes, slamming my lips against his. Surprise ricocheted a grunt through him, as he stumbled back a few steps.

Bryn responded with ferocity, plundering my mouth with his tongue, taking control of the kiss before I had a chance to. Letting go of my wrists, he slid his hands into my hair, tugging almost painfully. Wanting closer, I hopped up, wrapping my legs around his waist.

I ripped at his shirt.

He tore at my dress.

I yanked at his pants.

He removed my bra.

I freed him from his boxers.

He stole the last scrap of clothes from my body.

And then we were both naked, humming with need … and he found his home inside of me, there on the backseat of my car.

Teeth clashed, skin dripped with sweat, and magic swelled. It was bliss, and it was torture, the sweet agony of wanting it to end and to never stop.

I threw my head back, a kaleidoscope of colors

exploding behind my eyelids, a rainbow of satisfaction I would never grow tired of.

I could die here. In his arms.

"Fuck. Ta—lia. Lia, lia, lia … Fuck." Bryn spasmed inside of me, his entire body quivering as he found his own release.

Collapsing on top of me, he buried his face in my hair, against my neck. His hot breath caused me to shiver, goose bumps erupting in quick succession.

I closed my eyes. *What have we done? This should never have happened.* And yet, it had been glorious. Quite possibly the best five minutes of my life. Because our coupling had been fast, and animalistic … but completely satisfying.

I bit my lower lip. *Should I say something?* I opened my mouth, and shut it, only to open it again, before shutting it. *But what? What should I say?* How does one go about breaching such a subject with a sexy dragon … when he was still inside of you? I was pretty sure there wasn't an etiquette rule for my particular situation anywhere.

"Lia, baby. I can practically hear the wheels in that brain of yours grinding."

My eyes popped open. "Lia? What, we have sex once and you decide to rename me? And don't get me started on the whole baby thing."

"Not rename, nickname, completely different. If you don't like Lia, then how about …" He paused, a grin spreading across his face. "RU? Yeah, I like it."

"RU? What does it even mean?" At least Lia made sense.

"RU ... rainbow unicorn. Did you know your skin glows like a rainbow right before you come? But don't worry, I won't tell anyone. It'll be our little secret. And what? Should I wait until after we've done it a few more times to officially nickname you?"

I ignored his comment about my skin during sex, because no, I didn't know that. And he wouldn't be calling me anything but Talia. "A few more times?" I sputtered. "Nope. This time was a mistake, there won't be any others."

Propping himself up on his elbows, Bryn gazed down at me lazily, a smug grin twisting his lips up. "Really? You think this was a one time thing?"

"This isn't going to work, clearly. I mean, we're fighting ... still. We're still fighting and well, you're you know ... " I glanced down, and raised my eyebrows.

"You mean inside you? Yeah, I noticed." He swiveled his hips, his cock swelling to life again.

I gasped, hitting at his shoulders. "Don't do that. Stop it right now."

He rocked against me again. "Stop what?"

Biting back a moan, I dug my nails into his shoulders. "Bryn, please."

"Please what?" He nipped at my lower lip, stilling. "Keep going or stop?"

I bucked under him. "Keep going, you asshat. You just wanted to hear me say it."

Moving slowly, he pulled out, and slammed back in. I moaned. "Of course I wanted you to say it."

Pushing my knees to my chest, he shifted his angle, going even deeper. I hissed out a curse before biting his thumb as it swept across my face.

"I want to hear you say something else," he gritted out.

"Mmm," I grunted. *Why is he talking right now?* I was so close again already.

"Look at me."

I did, hoping it would shut him the hell up.

It didn't.

"RU, baby," he picked up the pace, and I dragged my nails down his back, "tell me you're mine."

"What?" I mumbled.

He leaned forward, his baby blues glowing brightly. "Tell me you're mine."

I answered him with a series of moans, which apparently didn't go over very well. He stopped moving.

"No!" I swatted at his ass. "You can't stop now!"

"Then tell me you're mine."

"Fine. I'm yours. Now— Unnnmaaugh." Coherent thought fled when he pivoted against me, pounding me over the edge again.

Fresh bliss settled over me ... just as pain seared the back of my neck. "What the hell?" Shoving at Bryn, I sat up. "What was that?" Using my magic to do an internal check, I found something foreign. Something ... "Holy shit! You did not do what I think you did."

But I knew. I knew just by the jubilant expression on Bryn's face that he had.

Covering the back of my neck with my hand, I glared daggers at him. "You did. You marked me as your *Anam Cara*."

His eyes blazed with pride. "Yeah, I did."

"How could you?" I clenched my fists against my thighs. "You tricked me! You used sex to force me into a commitment I didn't realize I was making. One I can't take back!" *Lie. Lie. Lie. You're lying to him and yourself. You knew exactly what you were agreeing to, and you let the moment carry you away. You wanted it—him. You want to keep him, despite your better judgment. He could actually be your soul mate.*

Yep, I knew a dragon could form the *Anam Cara* bond with a unicorn because our magic was compatible with any species. It was one of the things that made us unique. Plus, any child a unicorn conceived with another supernatural would always be born a unicorn. Its powers would simply be affected by the father. It was why our magic was like so many other species.

His smile faltered. "I thought you knew how it worked."

"I do. But," throwing my hands up in the air, I let them drop with a thump, "I didn't realize that's what was happening." *Lie.* "I mean, we had sex like once." *This is what you call buyer's remorse, Talia. It doesn't pay to let the sexy dragon claim you on impulse. Ugh. I'm seriously an idiot. He's not your soul mate. You just thought that because he was balls deep making you glow like a friggin' rainbow, apparently.*

"Twice."

I rolled my eyes. "Semantics. And that's not the point. I thought you said you didn't love me?" *Stop fighting it. Just tell him you wanted it in the moment, too. Tell him. Just tell him. Don't make him feel guilty.*

"I don't ... yet. But being with you, the way we were, my instincts took over."

I moved my hair over to cover my boobs. I didn't like the way my nipples were reacting to his gaze even though we were fighting. It was how I'd gotten myself into this mess to begin with. "And here I thought you were only half dragon," I muttered. *What's my excuse?*

Grimacing, Bryn exited the car. "Come on, we need to figure out what we're going to do about the demon infestation. We'll discuss the *Anam Cara* thing later."

I snorted. "Oh, now you want to figure the demon stuff out." Sliding out of the car, I grabbed my discarded clothes. "I'm going to go take a shower ... and think." I waved my hand dismissively at Bryn. "You stay here and think about what you've done."

"I'm not a dog you can order around."

"Are you sure you're not a dog, at least not a horny one? Because you certainly were all about humping my—"

"If I'm a horny dog then you're a cat in heat."

"Ugh. Again with the cat in heat? And that doesn't even make sense. Cats and dogs don't generally mate with each other. You don't make sense, Bryn." I ambled out of the garage, confusion draining my energy.

Of course none of this makes sense ... none of it at all. I mean, would I still be so confused if he was actually my soul mate? I don't even know anymore.

Chapter 16

Twisting around, I held up the hand mirror in front of the vanity, trying to get a look at Bryn's *Anam Cara* marking on the back of my neck. After a few seconds I was finally able to make it out. There, etched into my flesh, never to be removed unless Bryn left this mortal coil, was a huge black B with jagged edges.

"Fuck," I hissed. "I'm friggin' Bryn's *Anam Cara*." It was actually real. Never in my wildest dreams had I imagined being any dragon's *Anam Cara*. I had hoped that one day I would find and settle down with my soul mate, and maybe have a few mini-me's, but … but … *Fuck. I'm Bryn's Anam Cara. Hell of a downside to some explosive sex.*

I had absolutely no clue where to go from there. It had only been a few days since I'd even met Bryn, and here we were magically bonded forever. A concept that took on an entirely different meaning when both of us were practically immortal. And what happened if Bryn wasn't my soul mate, and I stumbled upon him down the line? What would that mean for any of us?

I've really messed things up this time.

I'd been angry at first, trying to convince myself that Bryn had tricked me into the bond somehow, but it was wrong of me to blame him. I knew from being raised by Daegus, that if Bryn's dragon instincts had screamed to claim me, and I hadn't dramatically protested ... well, it wasn't his fault. I'd decided to play with fire, welcomed the flames, and now I was suffering from third degree burns. *Okay, fine, it's mostly my fault. I did basically attack his face with my face, and yeah, act like a cat in heat.* He'd let his feelings be known, he'd obviously thought my sexual overture was my acceptance of our relationship. And it was ... until I grew regrets.

What am I supposed to do now? Just go with it? The optimist part of me figured that I might as well go with the flow and enjoy the delectable morsel of dragon fate had thrown at me. That it was all meant to be. That he had to be my soul mate. After all, I was insanely attracted to him, and now I'd have a true partner for life. But a minuscule part of me was a realist, and kept shouting that I was doomed. I'd only known Bryn for a few days, and what happened when the attraction wore off? When I found my true soul mate? What happened when it all became too much? I'd have no way out. I'd be trapped for life. *And damn if that voice isn't getting louder by the second.*

"Talia, darling! I need to get ready for a date," Maddie

sing-songed, pushing open the bathroom door, the one that had been locked.

My eyes met hers in the mirror. Dropping my hair, I spun. "M-Maddie," I stammered. "The door was locked. That's usually a sign that someone wants privacy. It's definitely not an invitation to, I don't know, pick the lock and force your way in."

Mouth hanging slightly open, Maddie stalked over to me, grabbing for my hair. "Wh-what was that? On the back of your neck?"

Skittering away, I clamped my hand over my neck, and forced a smile. "Nothing. Just a bit of dirt."

"That was not dirt." She grabbed at my hair again.

Slapping her hands away, I darted for the door, my heart thundering in my ears. "Go ahead and get ready for your date. I'll just wait out here."

Maddie dashed after me. "You get back here right now and tell me what's going on! You didn't—" Her voice dropped to a horrified whisper. "You didn't go and let that Neanderthal of a dragon claim you for his *Anam Cara*, did you?"

"Neanderthal? I thought you said he was hot and I should ride him like—"

"Sex is one thing, honey. But you never let them mark you. I mean, how long have you known him?" She clicked her tongue against the roof of her mouth. "Unbelievable. I should have known he was more trouble than you could handle. You're too innocent. Daegus kept you under lock and key like some fairy princess, which I guess you are, but still … maybe I should have taken Bryn off your hands."

I flung myself across my bed. "It's nothing. Just a spot of dirt." I didn't know why I was still attempting to deny it. Obviously Maddie knew exactly what she saw. I simply wasn't in the mood to discuss a lifetime bond with a mermaid who died a bit inside at just the idea of going on more than one date with the same male.

And take him off my hands? As if he'd be tempted so easily. *He's mine.* I resisted delving deeper into that irrational reaction. It was just the magic of the bond pushing me to be possessive.

Her fingers scraped along my neck, parting my hair. "Oh, honey, seriously? I was holding out hope that I was hallucinating."

Rolling over, I stuck out my lower lip. "I didn't realize what I was saying."

Her lavender eyes narrowed, sparking with anger. "You want me to kill him? I'll do it. Nobody tricks my friend into a—"

I waved my hands at her. "No! No killing. It was just a misunderstanding." My cheeks heated, the memory of the exact moment I'd lost myself to Bryn swirling through my mind. Why was I still lying to myself, and everyone else? Was it because I was embarrassed to have grabbed on to Bryn with both hands after only knowing him for a few days? Were we merely two lonely souls clinging to each other? And did it even matter if we were? In the end, the bond was formed, and we'd have to deal with the consequences. *Stop blaming the bond, and the magic. You wanted him, and you took him. Why should you feel ashamed? Instant connections can happen.* I swiped my hand down my face. *No. No, they don't. You're not in a damn romance novel. Things like that don't happen in real life ... do they?*

Realization hit me. *I don't believe in soul mates. All this time I've claimed I do, but I don't.* I was taught that every unicorn has one soul that fits perfectly with his or her own soul, but I'd never seen any proof. Not like the magical bonds forcing some other species together, for instance dragon *Anam Caras.* Or maybe I believed in soul mates, but not in the instant connection I was led to believe they would have. *Ugh. I'm just as bad as the humans, aren't I?* Could Bryn be my soul mate and I wasn't picking up on it all the way because I was determined to deny it? *Double ugh. Why is this all so complicated? Romance novels make it seem so easy. You meet your fated match on page one, and by page fifty you're happily settling into the honeymoon stage. Not like me who is considering moving to Siberia and not leaving a forwarding address for Bryn.*

"Misunderstanding?" Maddie reared back as if I'd slapped her. "You ... you aren't okay with this, are you?"

Nibbling the inside of my cheek, I considered. "No," I drawled. *Stop lying right now! What is wrong with you?* "Or yes." I flopped onto my stomach, burying my face in the comforter. "I don't know."

"Huh," Maddie grunted. "That must have been some sex to have you so twisted up. If it was me I would have ended him as soon as that mark showed up on my neck."

She drummed her nails, which resembled claws at the moment, across her thigh. "Nope, there is no male that gets to claim me and live to tell the tale."

Inhaling deeply, I tried to center myself. "Those are your issues, Maddie, not mine. I eventually wanted to settle down. This just happened a bit fast, and that's the part that has me all twisted up. Who's to say I wouldn't have ended up bonded to Bryn regardless of the timing?"

"How is it that feminism hasn't caught on yet in the supernatural world? I see so many dragons, wolves, and other female shifters delighting in the mate bonds. I get that magic is involved, but I don't understand why they—"

I sighed. This wasn't the first time Maddie and I had sparred over feminism. "How many times do I have to tell you, Mads? That's not what feminism means."

"I don't think *you* know what it means."

"Yes, I most certainly do. It means equality, and the ability to have choices, options. In this case, it means letting all females of any species decide what's right for them, what makes them happy. Not everyone wants the same things out of life, and we should all get to follow our own path without judgment." Flipping over, I pointed an accusatory finger at her. "In fact, your attitude is anti-feminist when you try to tell other females what they should or should not be doing."

She pursed her lips, and glared. "We'll have to agree to disagree."

"Whatever," I muttered, pulling myself into a sitting position. "I just don't get why—"

Darkness pushed around the edges of my vision, stealing the image of my room and Maddie. I whimpered, not wanting to face what I knew was inevitable ... again. And so soon.

Images ... images too horrible for me to comprehend skidded across my brain, forcing themselves upon me. I concentrated on focusing past those, past the death and mayhem, past the anger and fear, to what I needed to find. But it didn't work this time. I'd already linked with this demon—I'd already imprinted its energy signature on my psyche. And without that distraction, I fell full force into exactly what I always managed to avoid before ... the oozing black ichor of the demon's mind.

That's where I saw the children, and its plan. It was searching for me, targeting me, knowing that children would be my weak point ... because it knew what I was. I gasped, turning that knowledge over in my mind, diving deeper.

The demon knew about unicorns, and it was focused on me because ...

A female's vacant gaze stared up at the sky, blood pooling around her, turning her pink hair crimson. Her features were familiar, some of them having found their way onto my face.

Mom? As soon as I considered the idea, I knew it to be true. But I was seeing her through the demon's memory so she was distorted, different than the photos I'd seen of her.

Slender, masculine fingers reached out, grasping my

mother's chin, turning her head back and forth, as a plan formed. Laughter rang out. "Yes, I will find a way. Bring her."

Another demon resembling a walking, talking boulder, hefted my mother's limp body over its massive shoulder, grunting. "What do you want with a dead body, master?"

"This body is special. Very special. For it's the body of a unicorn, and I'm going to use it."

"But how? If you wanted the horn, you would have had to kill her in her other form. Everyone knows the horn is the best part."

"I have my ways."

I gasped, and everything went black.

Chapter 17

"**W**hat did you do to her?" Bryn's voice pummeled my eardrums even though it was barely above a growl. Faintly, through our new bond I could feel his anger, but below it, deeper, there was fear simmering.

"Me? I'm not the one who branded her, Neanderthal! It's probably the *Anam Cara* magic doing something to her! Maybe it's not compatible with her system!" Maddie yelled, a crash following a second later.

"It has nothing to do with our bond. Something's wrong. I sensed it. She should be awake by now. None of this is normal," Bryn hissed.

"Yeah, of course you sensed it because thanks to that little magical bond you forced on her, her emotions aren't even her own anymore."

"Guys," I rasped. "Seriously? Can you just … not." My

temples throbbed in time with my heart, my head seemingly filled with cotton candy.

"RU, baby, what happened? Tell me what you need." Bryn scooped me up in his arms, cradling me to his chest. My cheeks warmed at the use of his little nickname, conjuring images of us naked and entangled, which was his evil plan for calling me RU, I was sure.

"You could try not squeezing her to death," Maddie snapped.

I inhaled Bryn's unique and addicting scent, finding it comforting, which was a bit disconcerting. "Um, put me down, please." I didn't want to need him, and I wouldn't let the *Anam Cara* bond effect how I reacted to him. I could handle things on my own emotionally, just like I always did.

Reluctantly, Bryn placed me back on my bed. He leaned over me, pushing my hair out of my face as his glowing gaze searched my features. "Tell me what you need, please. I need to do something."

On its own accord, my hand snaked out to slide into his. *Shit. So much for handling things on my own.* Touching him, having contact with him in even such a small way, soothed the ragged edges from the vision I'd suffered through. *It's fine. Totally fine. We're partners. And partners rely on each other. Even Daegus would have comforted me.*

"I need to talk to Bryn alone, Maddie."

"You've got to be kidding me? Nope, not happening." She crossed her arms as her teeth lengthened and sharpened. I'd never witnessed her so agitated before. I'd heard the tales of mermaids transforming into a 'battle form', which included claws, fangs, and body armor type scales in place of skin, but I honestly didn't think I'd ever witness Maddie actually change.

Giving her a reassuring smile, I said, "You don't have to protect me from him, Maddie. He's my guardian, he would never harm me."

Her nostrils flared. "Says the female claimed as his *Anam Cara* against her will."

Black, iridescent scales erupted down Bryn's arms. "What we did was completely consensual. Don't make me out to be one of those archaic dragons who take their mates against their will."

"If the shoe fits," Maddie hissed, her skin pebbling with metallic scales of her own.

Jumping to my feet, I stood between them, hands outstretched. "Stop it, both of you. This isn't helping anyone, especially me." Marching over to Maddie, I poked her in the shoulder. "You don't get to decide what's between Bryn and me, okay? He's right. What happened between us was completely consensual. In fact, I'm pretty sure I instigated the whole thing." I glanced back at Bryn, who was watching me warily. "Sure, the whole mated for life bit was a tad of a surprise, and I could have done without getting asked right before orgasm number two, but I was raised by a dragon, and I know about how certain things work with *Anam Caras*."

"Coercion," Maddie interjected. "That's what it was then. And that's almost as bad."

"No." I poked her in the shoulder again. "A ... a misunderstanding. One I hope works out in the long run."

Maddie wrapped her arms around me in a hug. "You're not thinking clearly, Talia. You've been deprived of manly attention for too long, and you're acting a desperate fool."

"Hey!" I shoved her away from me. "Take that back! That was just rude and mean!"

"Again, if the shoe fits."

"That's it. I'm done dealing with your brand of crazy. Get out." I pointed at the door. "Now."

Maddie transformed back to her normal appearance, her head hanging. "I thought I was helping. You know I love you, right? You're like a sister to me."

My gut twisted. I loved her, too, but the closeness she felt for me, I didn't reciprocate. Keeping your true identity a secret had a way of erecting emotional walls. "Maddie, don't feel bad. You just have to understand that we don't look at the world the same way. For you, bonding for life is a death sentence."

"Yeah, for the guy," Bryn muttered. I skewered him with a death glare, instantly shutting him up.

Slinging my arm around her shoulder, I steered Maddie to the door. "Let me work this out with Bryn myself, okay? And next week we'll have a girls' night. We can talk about all the males you've been dating, and the slew of broken hearts you've left in your wake."

"I guess," she mumbled, pouting.

As soon as she was over the threshold, I shut the door, and locked it. "Cone of silence, cone of silence," I whispered, dancing in circle to fling the spell around my room. Maddie would probably immediately vacate the premises, but I couldn't risk her overhearing something if she threw me a curve ball and decided to eavesdrop.

"Cone of silence?" The corners of Bryn's eyes crinkled. "Is that what the spell is called or what you named it?"

"It's called cone of silence because I named it that. Deal with it."

Bryn sifted directly in front of me, all humor evaporating. "Now that she's gone, tell me what happened."

Heaving a sigh, I pushed him out of my way as I lumbered over to the bed. I flopped down, and pulled my knees to my chest. My heart quadrupled in time as I let myself recall what I'd seen when connected with the demon.

"You're trembling." Bryn wrapped his arms around me, enveloping me in warmth.

"I can't help it. I do this weird shaking thing when I'm upset or nervous. It's almost like I'm cold, but I'm usually not." I leaned into him, closing my eyes. "And what I saw …" My teeth started chattering. "I'm not even completely sure what I saw."

"I'm here." He kissed the top of my head, and tightened his grip around me. "And whatever it is, we'll deal with it together."

My chest tightened, and butterflies dive-bombed my stomach. He was well and truly my partner. Sure, the *Anam Cara* bond fostered closeness, forced our bodies to need to connect more often ... but I'd been inexplicably drawn to him from day one. Maybe he was indeed my soul mate—my soul had recognized his soul on some level, my magic knowing something I didn't want to admit. Was I pushing him away because of human sensibilities? Which would be ridiculous because I never had and never would be human. Had I wanted Bryn just as much as he wanted me, and I was afraid to admit it because of what it said about me? Afraid that it made me weak somehow?

Or was it all the *Anam Cara* magic trying to force me to accept Bryn? *Ugh. How will I ever know? And in the end, if I grow to love him, does it matter? Unless ... well, unless my true soul mate eventually shows up because Bryn isn't him.* I groaned.

Pushing all the *Anam Cara* and soul mate nonsense out of my mind, I forced myself to concentrate on the demon, and the horrible vision I'd been plunged into. "The demon, whichever demon it is ..." I shuddered, not wanting to say it out loud. Somehow my mother's body was involved, and the possibilities were revolting.

Bryn's lips moved softly against my hair as he whispered, "If you don't want to be my *Anam Cara*, if you think I tricked you somehow, then we can find a way to break the bond." He clutched me tighter, his fingers digging into my back. "Maybe a witch or something. I could die and be resuscitated. I'm not sure if it would work, but I'd be willing to try if that's what you wanted."

Squirming in his embrace, I pulled back enough to

stare up at him. "What are you even saying right now? You seemed so sure about things before." And talk about whiplash, something I was coming to expect from him. He wanted me to tell him about what happened, and as soon as I started he changed the subject completely. Not that I minded all that much at the moment.

"I would never want to force a bond on you that you either aren't ready for or didn't want at all. I may be dragon, but I'm also a guardian, and just the implication," he gritted his teeth, "does strange things to my insides."

Running my hand along his muscular arm, I leaned back into him. "Even though you're only half dragon, neither of us is human at all." I gnawed on the inside of my cheek. "You didn't force me, Bryn. And I'm not making up excuses or rationalizing away your bad behavior. We've had a sizzling attraction since we first met, and I tried telling myself that it would be a mistake for both of us to act on it."

Nuzzling him, I inhaled his scent, letting my eyes slide shut. "It would be easier to blame you for what happened between us, to hate you for it. To lie to everyone, including myself. Because I didn't, and still don't want to admit to anyone, especially myself, that I'm willing to risk it all for someone I barely know. I don't like the fact that sometimes if feels like I don't have any free will at all because of magic."

"Magic does complicate things." His fingers trailed down my spine in a winding pattern.

"What if we bonded because we were both lonely and starved for attention from the opposite sex?"

Bryn snorted. "I wasn't a virgin, RU. Not even close."

Sudden jealously burned through my veins. *Yep, there goes the Anam Cara magic at work.* Rationally I knew I had no claim to Bryn's past, and yet … "How many females have you been with?"

His chuckle rumbled low in his chest, vibrating against my ear. "Jealous? Don't worry, I never was even tempted to claim another female before I was inside of you."

"You never once thought about creating a bond with someone else? Not even for a millisecond?"

"Nope. Guess unicorns with blue hair just do it for me. Especially after they threaten to run me through with their horn."

"Dragons? Were they all dragons or did you venture outside of that gene pool?" Why did I care? His past with other females had zero relevance on our relationship. And yet I needed to know.

"Yes, they were all dragons."

"Hmm," I grunted. "What about long term girlfriends? Or were you only in it to get your rocks off?"

Bryn threw his head back, laughter erupting. "Do all these questions mean you're sure about being my *Anam Cara* now?"

I smacked his arm. "I'm not just your *Anam Cara*, you're mine. Got that? You, Bryn O'Bannon, belong to me, Talia White." Tapping my chin, I smirked at him. "At least for now."

His eyes widened. "For now? What's that supposed to mean?"

"I guess if I get sick of you, I could always get Maddie to end your existence. She'd probably even bury your body for me if I asked nicely."

"Not funny."

I grinned. "It is to me. But seriously ... let's give this *Anam Cara* stuff a shot. After all, like I said, we're not human, and it would be silly for me to apply their sensibilities to our situation." *Plus, what if you actually are my soul mate?*

I let my gaze travel over Bryn, my *Anam Cara*, a delectable dragon who I didn't have to keep my hands off anymore, or ever again. *Why did I think staying away from him was a good idea again?* I couldn't for the life of me remember why it wasn't the perfect plan to be partners on all levels, working together to hunt down demons. *Talk about a dream team.*

In that instant I came to a decision: I wanted to forget the vision, and the demon, and everything except Bryn, at least for the moment. My years had been filled with duty and demons, but nothing completely selfish ... until now.

I launched myself at Bryn, tackling him to the bed.

We could both die tomorrow, or the next day. The world was always uncertain, especially for a unicorn. So I was going to enjoy Bryn for a few hours today, simply because I could. *It's okay to be selfish once in a while, otherwise how will I keep going? How will I keep the world in balance if I'm broken?* And maybe that was the answer to everything right there. Had I been broken before Bryn had shown up, lonely and sad deep down, and he'd thrown me a life raft without realizing it? Was I in the process of fixing myself so I could go on to keep saving the world, smiting one demon at a time with him by my side?

Or was it just the *Anam Cara* magic bending me to its will? Not that any of it mattered anymore. Nope, all that mattered was Bryn was mine, and I was going to take full advantage of it while I could. I'd worry about the soul mate crap, and all the rest of it later. Much later.

"I need you," I moaned, tearing at Bryn's shirt.

"Yeah," he muttered, ripping my dress down the back. "Fuck, yeah. Me too. I mean, I need you, too."

The pulse between my legs screamed at me to ignore the torn dress even though I'd only worn it once. And I did ignore it, sort of. Even though I wouldn't stop touching Bryn, I couldn't resist verbally scolding him. "You better stop ripping my clothes or we're going to have a problem," I hissed between kisses.

"Simple solution: Be a nudist around me." His hands palmed my ass, squeezing.

"Whatever." Pressing my nose to his throat, I inhaled, humming in pleasure. My skin was burning, a raging fire of need, and Bryn's rough caresses were the only thing that could soothe me.

Lifting, Bryn impaled me from below, causing us both to cry out. "So fucking good," he growled, grinding his hips in a circular motion.

Dragging my nails down his sculpted chest, I moaned. "Faster, Bryn, faster."

"So demanding." Obeying, he picked up the pace, slamming into me.

"More. Bryn. More," I commanded, my voice raspy. Throwing my head back, I grabbed onto his muscular thighs, taking over the rhythm. He pressed his thumb against my clit, rubbing with just the right amount of pressure. My muscles tensed, my breath stuttering ... and then I was free falling into bliss as I screamed his name.

Collapsing across his chest, I mumbled a few nonsensical things, exhaustion tugging at me.

Flipping me over, still hard inside of me, Bryn flashed a feral grin. "We're not done yet. Not even close."

My body flared back to life as I stared up at the beautiful dragon looming over me. *How does someone like him even exist?* He was perfect in practically every way, like a fictional character invented just for me. "I heard dragons are insatiable," I purred, wrapping my legs around his waist. "Guess it's true."

"When it comes to you it's true." Leaning into me he snagged my lips with his, stealing all thoughts of anything but him.

Chapter 18

S played across Bryn's chest, I luxuriated in his warmth, and clean scent. "Can you shift into dragon form, since you're only half dragon?" I had so many questions for him, and I was attempting to get as many answered as possible while he was relaxed and willing. *Here's a tip: If you want honest answers from a man, human or supernatural, ask after he's come about a half dozen times. He'll never be more willing to talk.*

He ran his hands through my hair, tugging gently. "I can assume dragon form, but it's more difficult for me than full-blooded dragons. I have to expend more energy, although I can do it just as fast as them now." He expelled a long breath. "For a while I didn't think I'd be able to, my first shift wasn't until I was in my late twenties."

"Will you show me one day?" I drew little invisible circles on his pale skin. "I would love to see your other form."

"Only if you show me yours."

I nuzzled his neck, nipping playfully. "I guess it's only fair."

"I've never seen a unicorn in real life." He pressed a kiss to my forehead. "I bet you're beautiful in both forms."

"I like to think so." It wasn't me being vain or full of myself. I knew what I looked like. Unicorns were all stunning in their own way, and I'd gotten especially lucky in the gene pool. My human form was tall, lithe, and curvy in all the right places. My skin was creamy and smooth, the hair on my head a flattering aqua blue, and yet my body hair, like my eyebrows, was a normal shade of brown, matching my dark eyes. And, well ... my unicorn form was utter perfection. Golden horn, aqua mane, and rainbow-colored wings. Yep, I definitely didn't suffer from lack of self-confidence about my appearance. And frankly, I thought more females and males should celebrate themselves in all shapes and forms ... there's beauty in everyone who has a good soul because physical beauty is fleeting, which really made the body an insignificant part of what actually makes any creature appealing. *Why humans make it a crime to feel positive about themselves is beyond me. It's like if they don't constantly attack and try to improve their bodies then something is wrong with them. Very few of them nurture what's on the inside. Whatever. Humans are weird.*

A couple heartbeats of silence passed before he blurted, "Kids."

"Huh? What about them?"

"If we have kids, they'll be unicorns, won't they?"

Scrambling up, my mouth fell open. "Um … Kids? It's too soon to even think about that. We're still in the getting to know you phase of our relationship." Plus, they would only complicate things more if Bryn turned out not to be my soul mate.

Scooting back, I waved my arms around, my heart quadrupling in time. "I'm only thirty. I'll get back to you when I'm at least one hundred."

Shit. Shit. Shit. What if he wanted kids sooner rather than later? Hell, I didn't even know how old he actually was. What if he was entering into the stage where his dragon DNA pushed him to procreate? *Nope. Nopity, nope. Good thing a unicorn can't conceive unless she wills her body to ovulate. There will be no surprise or unwanted children growing in my womb.*

Bryn chuckled. "Calm down, RU. I'm not ready to be a father anytime soon. I guess I was just curious." His visage drained of all humor, his eyes sparking with flecks of bright blue. "I don't want any child of mine to go through what I did … not belonging anywhere."

"Oh." I inhaled and exhaled a few deep breaths, slowing my pulse. Bryn wanted information about possible future kids for a noble reason, not because he wanted to stick a bun in my oven post haste. "How bad was it for you? Growing up as a black dragon in a red clan? And being half guardian to boot?"

He ran his hands through his hair, flicking his gaze away. "I don't want you to get the wrong impression.

My adoptive parents did the best they could with me. It's just … " He swallowed, his Adam's apple bobbing. "I felt different all the time. Like I didn't belong. And I know it was mostly in my head. No one went out of their way to make me feel that way. But there were small … prejudices regardless. And yeah, some of them not so small at times." He sighed. "Until a few minutes ago, I thought I'd never have kids. And now that I have you, life is full of possibilities I never thought I'd get."

Diving at him, I wrapped him in a tight hug, burying my face against his neck. "Oh, Bryn. We can do anything we want together. Anything at all."

He clutched me tightly for a moment, then set me aside. "Except give up on hunting demons." He raised his eyebrows. "Don't you think you've stalled enough? Not that I'm complaining. Anytime you want to forget about something, feel free to use my body any way you want."

My cheeks heated. "You knew I was avoiding my vision and the demon stuff the whole time?"

"Of course." He tapped his temple. "Magical connection. I can practically read your mind."

"Well that explains some of what happened before …" Being so closely linked with Bryn definitely had its advantages, especially when it came to sex. "Why don't I feel you as strongly as you seem to me?"

"If you're hiding from your own emotions, what makes you think you're going to be good at finding someone else's?" He had a point. "Now, you ready to tell me about what you saw? I know it was traumatic, but we really do need to get back on track with this hunt."

"Well aren't you Mr. Responsible all of a sudden." Curling into his side, I closed my eyes, the image of my mother's dead body flashing across my mind. "Okay. Fine. I guess I can't avoid it forever." I shuddered. "The demon is targeting me. It knows what I am."

Springing to his feet, scales erupted down Bryn's naked chest and arms. "It knows you're a unicorn? Fuck. How did I not pick up on that part? We need reinforcements. We need," he pulled on his pants with jerky movements, "I need to contact every available dragon warrior from my clan. I have to— You should have told me this before we spent half the day in bed."

Stumbling to my feet, I grabbed at Bryn's arm. "Stop. It's part of why I wanted to spend so much naked time with you. I wasn't merely ignoring, I was—"

"Preparing for the worst." His fingers dug into my shoulders. "I'll die before I let anything happen to you."

Dizziness assaulted me, and I staggered back, Bryn's strong hands the only thing keeping me standing. Losing him after I was attached, it was one of the things I'd feared from the beginning, one of the reasons I thought distance between us was a solid plan. And now I'd gone and set myself up for exactly that—to possibly lose him. "Bryn, please, don't do anything to put yourself in danger."

"Better me than you."

"No!" I cried out, my voice shrill. "Please, promise me you won't put yourself in any unnecessary danger." He opened his mouth to respond, but I cut him off. "Promise me!"

He stared at me, his jaw muscles popping as he ground his teeth together. But he didn't promise. In fact, he didn't say anything at all, which was answer enough in itself.

I closed my eyes, diving deep into my reserve optimism, and yanking it over me, letting the warmth comfort and ease my tension. "It'll be okay. Nothing is going to happen to either of us. It'll all work out in the end, as long as we're careful. Very careful."

"You actually mean that, don't you? I could feel your anxiety and panic a moment ago, and now ..." He tucked my hair behind my ears, and I slitted my eyes to watch him. "Now you're serene. How'd you do it?"

"I'm a unicorn. Positive thinking is what we do. Besides, if I go into things thinking we're going to fail, then we probably will. Optimism is its own magic."

"You still have to finish filling me in on what exactly you saw, and how you want to proceed ... with things." He pulled me into his arms, tucking my head under his chin. "I'm falling for you, RU. Hard. And before you say anything, I know it's only been a few days since we met," his voice dropped a few octaves, "one of those filled with the best sex of my life, but this bond ... I understand why it fosters closeness. Being able to feel your emotions, being able to sense you the way I now can, I feel like you're the most essential part of me already."

I bit my lower lip, unsure of how to respond. He wasn't telling me that he could one day fall for me, like he had before. Instead he was letting me know that he was already there ... he was falling in love with me. I was both jubilant and terrified. My life no longer resembled the one I knew. Since the moment Bryn had sifted into my kitchen, things had gone crazy. I wasn't sure I'd begun processing what was happening between us. It still felt like an incredible dream ... and nightmare rolled into one.

I pulled away from him, pacing to my balcony door. Day was cresting into night, the sun skimming the horizon. Below on my lawn, Maddie sat cross-legged, glaring up at the door. I gasped, throwing it open. "How long have you been down there?"

Picking at a blade of grass, she frowned. "Not that long, I suppose." She leaned back on her elbows, arching her bikini-clad body towards the last remnants of light.

"It's a wonder to me that you never get cold," I muttered, before clearing my throat. Of course mermaids could usually be found in next to nothing year round, their magic protecting them from the cold on land and in the water. "Why are you there? Waiting and lurking?"

She clicked her tongue. "Just wanted to make sure you didn't need me to help you bury the body."

"Are you serious?" Bryn moved in behind me, wrapping a thick, purple robe around me, staving off my shivers. *Huh. Wonder where he got it from? Guess he could have sifted to a store real quick. Handy indeed.* I'd never considered the possibilities with Daegus because he would have laughed in my face if I asked him to pop here or there on a whim, but with Bryn. *Hmm ...*

Not even sparing Maddie a glance, Bryn retreated to my room. "Don't be too long, we have ... work to do."

I shoved my hands in the robe's pockets. I'd still somehow avoided sharing the entire story of what I'd seen in my vision. I knew I had to get back to tell him, and I would, as soon as I dealt with Maddie. "So, you didn't really think I'd kill him, did you?"

Maddie shrugged. "A girl could hope." The corner of her mouth twisted up. "At least he's stuck with a ... unique *Anam Cara* mark on his neck."

I couldn't help but laugh. While I had a plain black mark on the back of my neck, Bryn was adorned with a jagged T in a rainbow of colors. All the colors, in fact. It even glittered when the light hit it. I grinned. Our *Anam Cara* brands were just another sign of how my magic would make us an anomaly as a pairing. I couldn't wait to find out what else would differ from other *Anam Caras*. *Please let him turn out to be my soul mate so I can keep him forever.*

I sniggered. "Yeah, that was a surprise."

Maddie narrowed her eyes. "The real reason I'm here." She glanced left and then right. "You're not really a fae princess, are you? You're—"

Bryn appeared in front of her, slamming a hand over mouth. "Shut up," he hissed. "You never know who's listening."

"Bring her inside, now," I snapped, whirling around.

Great. Someone else knew what I was. I'd gone thirty years without anyone finding out my secret, and within twenty-four hours I discovered my cover was blown ... twice.

The thing was ... All I had to do was kill the demon and its mouth would be permanently shut. But with Maddie, could I trust her with my true identity? And if I couldn't ... then what?

Welp, for the longest time I wished people could get to know the real me. I should have known to always be careful what you wish for, especially when you're a unicorn.

Chapter 19

"Bryn, this is completely unnecessary." I crossed my arms, and glared at him. He astutely ignored me, standing behind Maddie with a dragon blade clutched in his hand, ready to strike at any moment.

He'd managed to get Maddie into the house, and tie her down to one of the chairs in the kitchen. She hadn't put up much of a struggle, which told me oodles in itself. She wanted to talk, despite the mutual dislike blooming between her and Bryn, aka they wanted to kill each other ... literally.

"Neanderthal, just like I said." Maddie seemed unconcerned with the current threat on her life, which was also telling. Mermaids were often underestimated magically, and I knew Bryn would do just that if it came down to an actual battle.

Crouching in front of my friend, I rested my hands on

her knees and stared up into her lavender eyes. "He's just being cautious. Can you understand why now?"

She licked her lips, the first sign of nerves, as she leaned forward, her features pinched. "I thought unicorns were wiped out completely, on this plane and all others." She shook her head. "No wonder I feel drawn to you, and the need to protect you. It's almost a compulsion."

"Yes, supernatural creatures are often drawn to me and they don't know why. It's completely natural."

"It's more than that," she said. "Every time I consider leaving your land, something keeps me here. I need to be here, and now I know why. It's to help protect you."

"I'm her guardian, and I don't need your help," Bryn growled, inching closer to her.

I raised my hands. "Bryn, seriously, chill. If she wants to protect me, then she obviously isn't a threat. Put the damn sword away before you do something you'll regret."

"I wouldn't regret ending her. Not if it means keeping your secret safe in order to protect you, like I pledged to do."

I conjured my best wounded animal eyes. "*I* would regret it. Maddie is my friend."

Bryn cursed under his breath, dematerializing the dragon blade. "This *Anam Cara* bond is going to be inconvenient at times like this when I know what I should do, but can't because it'll cause you pain."

I grinned. "Then maybe you should have thought of that before you were loose with your lips while—"

"Okay, enough," Maddie snapped. "I really don't want

to witness another round of foreplay between you two. Fighting seems to be your thing." She rolled her eyes. "How cliché."

Scowling, I crouched back down in front of Maddie. "Be nice or I won't cook for you anymore."

"Ha!" Bryn barked out.

I pointed at him. "You either." His lower lip jutted out, and I resisted the urge to kiss it away. *Damn hormones.* They needed to chill more than anything else.

Maddie cleared her throat demonstratively and clicked her tongue. "As I was saying, the reason I'm drawn to you is more than you being a unicorn. My great, great, great grandmother several times over was the Lady of the Lake. My line has been tasked with helping to keep balance. The very same balance—"

"Unicorns are born to do." I studied my friend closely, realizing maybe I didn't know her any more than she knew me. *Surprise, surprise.*

"Yes," she said. "And I've also been tasked with guarding Excalibur."

My eyes widened. "Excalibur. *The* Excalibur?"

"The one and only."

"Dragon blades are better," Bryn scoffed.

Maddie rocked back and forth in the chair, incensed. "Please! Excalibur is sentient. He can feel, make his own choices, and wield his own magic if need be. How is a dragon blade better than that? They're nothing more than metal infused with magic. Your blade may be deadlier than a regular sword, but it's no Excalibur."

Bryn grumbled under his breath, turning towards the fridge, digging around for food.

"Can I see it?" I bounced up onto the balls of my feet, clapping. "Excalibur, I mean. Can I see it?"

"You get distracted so easily," Bryn mumbled around a mouthful of pie. "Focus, RU. Focus."

"Said the dragon with a mouth full of pie."

Shrugging, he shoved several more bites into his mouth, puffing his cheeks out. "Can't think straight on an empty stomach."

Maddie grimaced. "I hate to agree with the Neanderthal, but you do need to focus. I'm here for a reason, and that reason is you. I just didn't know it until now. I think you might be the next owner of Excalibur. Which means you're stuck with me."

A plate clattered to the floor, breaking into smithereens. "Ah, hell no," Bryn growled. "You have already worn out your welcome."

"I'm a package deal with Excalibur. If the sword belongs to Talia, like I think it does, then I have to hang around to guard her and it. I don't make the rules, the magic does."

"Bryn, untie her. Regardless of whether or not Excalibur is mine, it's pretty clear Maddie isn't going to run around telling people about me." I could have easily untied her myself, but I wanted Bryn to do it to make a point.

He shuffled across the floor, dragging his feet. With a flick of his wrist, he set Maddie free. "Happy?" he muttered, retreating to the closet to fetch a broom to clean up the broken plate.

Maddie rubbed the red marks on her wrists, healing them instantly. "Of course I would never run around telling people about a unicorn, even if I wasn't friends with you." She stared at me with amazement. "I still can't believe it took me all this time to figure it out."

"Why now? Why after all this time did you figure it out?"

"Ever since Neanderthal showed up," she pointed at him, her face scrunching up with disdain, "you've been different. Then there was the fancy *Anam Cara* mark on his neck. Couple that with the glyph on his chest … well, when I saw that, I just knew. Maybe something in me recognized the magic? Not sure."

"I'd appreciate it if you stopped calling him Neanderthal. I kind of like him. At least enough to keep him around for a while." Images of our naked limbs entangled swirled through my brain, heating every molecule in my body. *Damn, no wonder newly bonded Anam Caras usually stayed in seclusion for months. No.* I shook my head. Although infinitely more appealing than a demon hunt, I couldn't shirk my responsibilities any longer.

Maddie kicked her legs up on the kitchen table, tilting the chair back onto two legs. "Looks like I'm part of the squad now."

My eyes bugged out as a huge grin split my face. I glanced at Bryn, and he shook his head. "She's not going to want it either," he grumbled.

Maddie's gaze darted between the two of us. "Want what?"

"Team Unicorn Talia! You're on my team now so you have to have the shirt!" Dashing upstairs, I made quick work of finding it.

Once back in the kitchen, I thrust it at Maddie. "For you."

Holding it out in front of her chest, she wrinkled her nose. "You don't expect me to actually wear this, do you?"

Sinking to the floor, I covered my face with my hands, groaning. "Why doesn't anyone want it? It's so adorable."

Maddie patted the top of my head as she stood. "It's cute, but I'm not five." Sashaying her way to the door, she glanced back at me. "Well, come on. I thought you wanted to see Excalibur."

"Hell yeah!"

"RU," Bryn yelled. "We don't have time for this right now."

Sticking my tongue out at him, I sprinted through the open door, eager to find out if the legendary sword was mine.

Fine, I'm avoiding the demon issue again. I still haven't figured out what to do with my magic seemingly on the fritz. But come on ... it's friggin' Excalibur we're talking about here.

Chapter 20

I crinkled my nose. "It doesn't look like I thought it would." Instead of the gleaming silver sword etched with intricate ancient symbols I thought I'd find, Excalibur resembled a rusty artifact.

Maddie flipped her long hair over her shoulder, sighing heavily. "He's definitely seen better days. But I was assured once he found his new owner he'd be as good as new." She brushed her fingertips along the dull blade, and then stared down at the lake. "How, I'm not exactly sure."

"It's a piece of crap," Bryn coughed out into his fist, averting his eyes to stare off into the woods.

"Subtle," I said, smacking at his massive arm. He smirked, not repentant in the least.

"Well, you want to try holding it?" Maddie thrust Excalibur at me, a hopeful gleam in her eyes.

The forest seemed to hold its breath as I reached for it. As soon as my fingers wrapped around the hilt, a blinding light burst from Excalibur, knocking me on my ass. Heat suffused my system as unfamiliar magic filled me to the brim. I couldn't look away, couldn't move—couldn't anything except stare at the blazing majesty clutched in my hands.

"RU! Can you hear me? Tell her to let go!" Bryn's desperate voice reached my ears, but I was enthralled.

My head buzzed, as if something was trying to communicate with me, and that's when I understood. It was Excalibur, he wanted in my mind, needed to know me to see if I was indeed his new master. "Go ahead," I murmured, "you have my permission."

More magic flooded me, spilling over, consuming everything ... so bright. Brighter than anything I'd ever seen, illuminating everything inside of me. But it was too much. I was ripped open, drowning in my own power.

Sweat dribbled down my spine, and my toes curled, my bare feet digging into the dirt. I swayed, confusion settling over me. I wasn't sure what was happening, or even who I was anymore.

No, that's not true. I'm Talia White, bringer of love and joy, peace and balance. For I am unicorn.

Everything went dark.

"WHOEVER'S TAP dancing on my head needs to stop." Groaning, I blinked my bedroom ceiling into focus.

"RU, baby," Bryn said, appearing in my line of sight.

His eyes were lit up like two flashlights, making his face seem hollowed out and severe. "You're okay."

"Of course she's okay. I told you she would be," Maddie said, her voice wafting over from somewhere on my right. "Excalibur chose her. Which is a good thing, although a shock to the system from what I understand."

Wiggling the fingers of my right hand, I felt something solid and heavy. "Excalibur," I murmured. I sensed him, simply knew it was him. There was a link between us now, like an invisible golden thread, tethering us together. And although Excalibur didn't speak in words, I somehow understood him on a visceral level.

I snorted, and sat up. "Two unexpected bonds within the last couple of days. I've been a busy unicorn." My gaze slid down to my new sword, and I sucked in a surprised gasp. It was absolutely beautiful, and nothing like the rusted antique I'd first taken hold of. Instead, a gleaming silver katana, with an intricate rainbow and stars pattern on the hilt, gleamed up at me. "Umm ... this is not the same sword."

The bed dipped beside me under Maddie's weight. "Nope. Excalibur changes to fit its owner. Guess a katana is the best sword for you." Her fingers hovered over the hilt. "And I should have figured you'd find some way to work rainbows and stars into the design." She shook her head.

"I didn't actually forge the new version of Excalibur myself as you well know, smartass. I guess he just knew rainbows and stars suited me." Lifting my new prize, I swiped it through the air. "It is lighter and easier to manage than a claymore, a broadsword, or even a dragon blade." I smirked at Bryn.

He settled on the other side of me, throwing his arm around my shoulders so he could pull me into his side. "Yes, because you've been around so many swords in your lifetime. I'm surprised you even know what a claymore or a broadsword is."

"Shut up. There are plenty of things you don't know about me yet." I certainly wasn't going to tell him that I only knew a few sword names from reading historical romance, and from a movie here and there.

"Do you think I can materialize and dematerialize Excalibur like dragons do with their swords?"

Bryn quirked one dark eyebrow. "Can you sift?"

Disappointment nettled. "Damn, how am I supposed to carry it around with me then? Humans usually frown upon huge pointy weapons in public." I sliced Excalibur through the air again, mesmerized by his beauty. He didn't want to be left behind any more than I wanted to leave him. "I suppose I can glamour him."

"What are you going to do with a sword anyway?" Bryn asked. "You don't even like the sight of blood, and now you're going to carry it around with you everywhere … just because?"

I shrugged. "For emergencies?"

Bryn tapped my nose. "That's what I'm here for."

Glaring at him, I ground my teeth together. I hated that he had a point. Why did Excalibur choose me? Sure, as a unicorn I was powerful, but I wasn't the katana wielding type, even if I wished I could be. But I wasn't going to look a gift horse in the mouth and simply toss him aside. I'd figure out the reason he'd attached himself to me ... eventually.

The sudden chime of the doorbell startled me out of my reverie. "Huh. I wonder who that could be?" Climbing over Bryn, I padded across the floor. "I'm not expecting anyone."

"Might want to leave the sword here," Bryn said, "until you have the glamour up and running if you insist on toting that thing around."

I handed Excalibur to Bryn. "Good point."

"Hey!" Maddie exclaimed. "He shouldn't be able to touch it."

I shrugged. "Probably something to do with us being *Anam Caras* now. Our bond is a bit wonky, so who knows."

Shuffling down the stairs, I smiled to myself as I made my way to the front door. I could officially add one more person to my list of true friends. Of course Bryn was technically more than a friend, but that part didn't matter. For the first time in my life, I felt ... not alone. Deeply and truly, not alone.

Swinging my front door open, I was greeted by a group of smiling Girl Scouts, about six of them. "Hi," I said. "Is it that time of year again?" *But wait, that isn't right.* Girl Scout cookie time started in January, didn't it? I scratched the side of my head, and smiled. Maybe they were expanding cookie time or starting early? *Huh. And they usually don't come in such a big group either.*

A small girl in the front with dreadlocks grinned, exposing braces. "Can we come in to talk to you?"

I tilted my head. "Come in? To talk to me about what exactly?" Something was definitely wrong with this situation; I just couldn't put my finger on what.

"Ads," another girl in the back chimed in, her red hair in two long braids that stuck out like Pippi Longstocking. "We want to talk to you about buying ads for our Girls Scout online publication."

"You have an online publication? That has ads?"

"Yes, exactly." The first girl nodded vigorously. "We just want to come in to talk about your options and to see if you'd be interested in sponsoring our troop."

Oh, okay. So their entire troop is on my doorstep. Things were making a bit more sense. And what did I know about the workings of modern Girl Scouts? "Come—" The rest of the invitation lodged in my throat, as if my body was rebelling against the words. I backed up a few steps, retreating farther into my house. "Now really isn't a good time girls. Just leave any pamphlets or information in my mailbox and I can look at it later." I slammed the door shut, internal alarm bells reverberating in my skull.

Tiny fists pummeled my front door. "Let us in. It'll only take a minute."

Peering out my peephole, I saw several pairs of eyes flash red. *Holy shit!* I'd taken so long tracking down the demons that they'd come to me. *But how did they manage to find my house? It has so many wards on it. Unless …*

"Let us in! Let us in now!"

I couldn't decide if it was ironic or not that the Girl Scouts turned out to be demons. After all, even the human versions sold crack in the form of cookies. Shaking my head to dislodge the whimsy, I did a quick scan of said wards, shocked at my findings. "Bryn!" I yelled. "We have a major problem!"

He sifted to the bottom of the stairs, rushing over to me. "What's wrong?"

"The wards aren't working properly. Only the ones to physically keep unwanted guests out are still intact." I gulped. "The rest …" I shook my head.

His eyes darted to the door in understanding. "You've been exposed."

Maddie thundered down the stairs. "It must have been Excalibur. Too much magic can overload wards." She smacked her forehead. "I should have known better. I've had the same kind of protection spells up, and I felt them come crashing down earlier. I should have told you to check yours." She sidled up to the door, peeking out at my prepubescent assailants. "Demons? I thought the old stories of unicorns tracking demons was a myth." She scrunched up her nose. "And are you sure they're demons? I don't sense demonic energy from them. "

"Yes, they're demons. But ones that even I can't sense. And if you want to be part of Team Unicorn Talia you need to pay attention, Mads! What do you think I've been stressing over?"

"I don't know—your new dragon guardian, your *Anam Cara* bond with him, and the discovery of Excalibur, just to name a few things."

"None of that matters now. We need to ... I don't know!" Wringing my hands together, I started pacing. The smart thing would be to have Bryn sift me to his dragon clan until we found a new suitable place to live, and had new wards up and running. But my house was my safe place, my sanctuary. And I didn't want to live anywhere else. Plus, when on clan lands I lost my connection to demons. Too much dragon magic and wards for me to sense around.

This is the price you pay for shirking your responsibilities. You should have been doing nothing but trying to figure out why your magic didn't work before. I'd been tracking demons since I was a teenager. It was a job I'd become complacent about, bored almost. I would deal with the nasty denizens of Hell in my own time, knowing that I couldn't stop them from destroying and maiming to a certain extent. It was my way of protecting my psyche, knowing that there would be casualties no matter what I did, and that is was all part of the grand plan. The most important part was keeping myself alive and in good spirits so I'd be around for future jobs. *But now this demon has made it personal, and I'm pissed.*

Bryn grabbed me around the waist. "I need to get you out of here. We can figure out the rest later."

"No," I snapped. "I will not be chased out of my home." Nibbling my lip, I glanced at the door. "Maybe I should try using my magic again. I could have been drained before, and I have had a chance to recharge."

"Not even a pinky toe steps outside of this house," Bryn said, reluctantly releasing me.

"Don't worry, I'm not risking it." *Let's get this over with. It'll probably be fine now. You can do this, just like the thousands of times you have before.*

Flinging the door open, I doused the air with magic, an explosion of golden dust settling over each Girl Scout. Red eyes continued to blink at me.

I slammed the door. "Shit. Why isn't it working? I don't understand. I don't feel like I'm drained on any level."

Maddie grimaced. "Being that you can't exorcize them with your magic, unless you want to mow down all those little girls with Excalibur then … he's right. Live to fight another day and all of that."

"No," I snapped again. "I said, I will not be chased out of my home."

Digging my nails into Bryn's forearms, I spoke through clenched teeth. "Take me to the senator's house."

"Have you lost your mind? You magic isn't working. You're too vulnerable without your powers."

"You're just going to have to be extra good at protecting me then." His nostrils flared, but before he either obeyed or argued, I remembered Excalibur. "Maddie, I'm probably going to need my sword." Without my magic working properly, maybe Excalibur had come to me now for a reason.

"On it!" She hustled up the stairs to retrieve my new weapon.

Not meeting his gaze, I patted Bryn's shoulder. "Don't worry. This time I actually have a plan."

And hopefully by the time we found the head demon, the plan would be more than a plan to have a really awesome, kickass plan. Especially since my magic was still on the fritz.

Chapter 21

I 'd messed up. I could admit it. I'd become too complacent about tracking demons, letting my guard down. Now I was exposed and vulnerable for the first time in my adult life, stripped of magic, my ace up the sleeve in the battle against evil.

But at least I wasn't alone.

Clutching Excalibur, I skirted around the side of the senator's huge brick house, Bryn to my right brandishing his dragon blade, and Maddie to my left in full mermaid battle armor.

"I'm still against this plan," Bryn muttered as he shuttered his eyes to keep the glow from alerting anyone to our presence. Luckily it was daytime, and the grounds seemed deserted.

"No one asked you, Neanderthal," Maddie hissed around fangs.

I shuddered. I loved her and all, but mermaids were

seriously terrifying in full armor. They were something right out of a horror movie. *Good thing she's on my side.*

"Play nice," I commanded. "Now is not the time for bickering within Team Unicorn Talia's ranks."

"Stop calling us that!" Bryn and Maddie said in unison.

"Well, at least you two can agree about something." I smiled brightly. "And yes, we are Team Unicorn Talia, so deal with it."

Bryn pressed his shoulder up against mine as I paused to peer into a window. "What are we even doing here? Clearly the demons are tracking you now. They know you can't exorcize them. Coming here was—"

"The only thing I could think of in a pinch. I'm not used to things being ... so complicated. I guess my instincts are out of whack and in desperate need of practice in weird scenarios."

Bryn's brow wrinkled. "You just admitted your instincts are out of whack and we're supposed to follow you?" He reached for me, and I sidestepped him. "Let's just go to my clan. We can figure everything out in a safe and protected environment."

Maddie tapped her chin with long claws. "Would I get to come along? Because if I do, I'm not mad at his idea if it includes me and a bunch of sexy, single dragons."

I sighed. "Really, Mads? Really?"

She shrugged. "Us single ladies like to keep our options open."

"I didn't expect to find you skulking around here after I sent my minions to your home," a male voice came from behind us. "Unicorns are odd creatures, and not entirely intelligent from what I can tell."

I hung my head. *Shit.* We'd done the classic, and completely asinine move of being so caught up in our own conversation, we didn't notice someone walking up behind us. A demon no less. Smacking my palm to my forehead, I only then noticed the telltale burn. *Seriously, I'm so off my game.*

Whirling around, the three of us dropped into battle stances. Me swaying slightly because, well, I'd never actually used a sword before. *It can't be too hard, right?* Excalibur hummed in my palm, as if he was encouraging me. I nodded. *Thanks. I'll do my best. And I promise to train with you if we make it out of this in one piece. You know ... for emergencies like this one.*

"RU," Bryn hissed, "the demon is talking to you."

"Huh?" I glanced up from Excalibur. "Oh, sorry. Can you repeat that?"

The demon's full lips curled back in his near perfect face. I'd never seen a demon, male or female, who wasn't inhumanly stunning. Unlike in most stories, on and off screen, true evil always hides behind beauty because it doesn't like to advertise itself. One thing Hollywood got right though—the villains, especially demons, loved to monologue. This demon was no exception, with his perfectly quaffed blond hair, and his flawless complexion.

He straightened his tie, drawing my attention to his expensive looking suit. I fought the urge to roll my eyes at yet another cliché. Yep, demons loved the finer things in life, especially when topside in the human realm.

"Go on, you were saying?" I mocked.

This—this type of interaction was what I was used to. What had my stomach in knots was not knowing what had been done with my mother's body all those years ago, and how exactly this demon had used her to connect with me. He was a powerful bastard though, which I could tell simply from the fact that he'd taken his true form, and hadn't needed to possess a human.

"Is it really a good idea to torment the demon?" Bryn hissed, inching his way in front of me. "Say the word and I'll end him." As he should, my dragon was waiting for the nod to take our foe's head. It was my job to decide when to let him off his leash, in case there was anything I needed to do first, such as get pertinent information about my mother's body.

"Meh, it's fine." I motioned to the demon, waving him on. "Go ahead, tell us all about your dastardly plan. We don't have all day."

His eyes sparked red, his features pinching. "Were you dropped on the head as a baby?"

"Excuse me?" I shimmied in front of Bryn, who scowled down at me. "You did not just imply that I was brain damaged."

The demon flicked invisible lint off his suit. "I did indeed."

"What is that smell?" Maddie interjected, coughing into her hand. "That—that's rank."

Lifting my nose, I inhaled, getting a whiff of death and decay. Gagging, I covered my mouth and nose with my free hand, bile burning my throat. "What is that? Didn't your mother teach you to clean up after yourself?" I didn't even want to consider what could be causing the foul stench.

"Maybe we should ask your mother what she thinks about my habits?"

"What? That doesn't even make sense, you—" My heart plummeted to my feet, before twisting out a staccato rhythm of anguish. "No," I gasped, "it can't be!"

Making its way around the corner, ambled the broken and rotting body of my mother, or rather what was left of her. Skin hung off in clumps, exposing rotting bone and withering muscle. White milky eyes met mine, shimmering red. Her mouth opened, moving out of time with the words that came from within her. "Hello, my darling. I've missed you so."

Focusing on my mother's corpse, I used my magic to scan her body. It buzzed with demonic energy, dark and sinister, but none of my mother's soul left in tact. Exhaling a shaky breath, relief washed over me; a cool, soothing balm. It was a sacrilegious violation to desecrate her so, to keep her body all these years, but her spirit had moved on, and to me that was the most important thing.

Lifting Excalibur with one hand, I pointed at the demon. "That's just a bag of bones filled with demonic energy. My mother's spirit is gone." I ground my teeth together. "But I'm still going to make you suffer for what you've done."

"Ah, but her flesh has done its job, so I've already won." The demon snapped his fingers, and my mother's body dropped to the ground, disintegrating into a pile of dust, the stench of it lingering.

"You've won nothing," I snarled. I still wasn't sure how'd he'd used my mother's corpse to forge a connection to me, or what the point to reanimating it had been. Unless he'd simply done that for my benefit on the spur of the moment to throw me off balance.

"I have you now, a living, breathing unicorn. It's a prize I've waited thousands of years for."

He waved his hand, sending Bryn and Maddie vaulting backwards through the air. Mid flight, Bryn sifted in front of me, a roar erupting from him as he dashed forward. Flames crackled to life around the demon as he formed a protective circle for himself.

Glancing over my shoulder, I heaved a sigh of relief when I spotted Maddie on her feet, uninjured.

"Come out here and fight me!" Bryn bellowed as he swiped his blade into the flames, and dragged it back several times.

The demon grinned. "I'm perfectly fine in here. After you tire out, I'll kill you and take my prize." His gaze flicked to me.

"Like hell you are." Bryn continued his dance around the flame circle, making me wonder what in the world he was doing. He had to know he didn't have a chance of—

And then I saw it. A steady stream of water making its way over the hill, and pooling around Bryn's feet. *Duh. Water dragon.* He was obviously causing a diversion while he put his real plan into action.

Moving forward, I let my horn shift into existence on my forehead, knowing it would catch the light of the fire, and be exceedingly distracting to a demon coveting exactly what I was showing off.

The demon's eyes glinted, focused fully on me. "So wonderful," he murmured.

A wave of water crashed down around him, dousing his protective circle. Bryn sifted in, a triumphant smile adorning his face, even as the demon threw a fireball at him. Sifting in and out, Bryn dodged the flames shooting his way, getting closer and closer. Demons weren't nearly as badass or powerful as they thought they were, at least none I'd ever gone up against. I'd put money on a dragon warrior any day. It was only a matter of time before Bryn ended him.

I ground my teeth together, wanting to help Bryn. Needing on some level to be the one who snuffed out this particular demon's existence. This wasn't a normal hunt. No, because this demon had desecrated my mother's body. It was Bryn's job to make any and all kills. It was done for a purpose, since although a unicorn could be fierce when need be, it simply wasn't in our make up to kill for any reason. We protected life, not took it. Despite my nature, I needed this one, had to have it.

Excalibur lit up with a golden light, vibrating in my

hand. Without thought I dashed forward, swiping at the demon, the blade gliding through his neck like butter while he faced Bryn. I danced back in time to witness shock registering, his mouth forming a small circle of surprise, before his head toppled to the ground, his body lying in two separate pieces.

"Nothing!" I screamed. "You won nothing, and are nothing now!" I punted his head, sending it up into the air a few feet before it hit the ground with a sick thud. "Nothing!" I screamed again.

What he'd done to my mother had been—something I wasn't coping very well with now that the immediate threat was gone. I was spiraling into a dark abyss, a place unicorns didn't usually go. We all had dark and light inside of us, but a unicorn's light overwhelmed the dark, which was the natural state of things for us. But seeing the zombified corpse of my mother—it had snapped something in me, and I wanted—

I want revenge. The unfamiliar emotion gurgled to life within me, spreading like a virus, making me sick.

Strong arms banded around me, turning me away from the demon. Excalibur thudded to the ground. "RU, shhh, I've got you. Come on, RU, baby, I've got you." Bryn's comforting embrace grounded me, yanking me out of the murky ichor, pulling me towards the light. He warm lips touched the top of my head, as he murmured, "I'm right here for you. Whatever you need, I'll do it."

Inhaling his clean scent, I nodded against his chest. My moment of weakness had passed, and slowly I came back to myself, letting go of my anger. *The demon's dead. Move on.* "We need to take a look around inside to see if he left any clues behind." I wrapped my arms around Bryn's waist, finding the energy to hug him back. "I let my temper get the best of me and now we don't know what he was up to. We need to figure it out and then clean up his mess." *I've never killed anyone, not even a demon before. Will it change me? Am I already different? No. It'll only change you if you let it, and you won't. You can't.*

Bryn stroked my hair. "Exorcising the children of their demons should be easy now that their master is gone, right?"

I grimaced. "Not exactly. They're going to be like mogwais fed after midnight, turning into gremlins and reeking havoc without any kind of plan. If I'd been thinking straight I would have done things differently." Or if I'd been thinking at all. "This whole thing has been a huge mess since day one."

"Yeah," Bryn muttered. "And I didn't even get to make my first official kill. You're the tracker, remember? As in you track down the demon, and I kill it."

I smacked at his back without letting him go. "I've been trained since practically birth to be able to take a demon down myself if I had to, so—"

"If you had to in order to protect your life, and with me here you don't. Plus, you work with your magic, not an ancient sword."

Breaking away from Bryn, I scooped up Excalibur. "Thank you for helping me." He buzzed, flashing gold, which I took as a 'you're welcome'. Sheathing him at my back, I glanced over at Maddie, who was sitting cross-legged on the lawn playing with her phone. I cleared my throat.

She jerked her head up. "What? You two were having a moment, and I didn't want to interrupt. Plus," she flicked her hair over her shoulder, "I was making plans for a date later."

"I thought you wanted to help me with the demons."

She raised her eyebrows. "We're not going to be done by dinnertime?" She sighed. "This is an exhausting job. Maybe you should think about retiring."

"Sure, I can retire, after another hundred or so years." If I was lucky.

"We don't need your help anyhow," Bryn interjected.

"Yes, we do." I poked him in the side. "The more the merrier I'd like to think when it comes to hunting down spawns of Hell."

Bryn grunted. He couldn't exactly argue, even though he wanted to. We had our work cut out for us with the dozens of possessed children we had to first find before exorcizing … somehow. Hopefully with the head demon dead, my magic would actually do the job, unlike before.

Placing my hands on my hips, I stared down at the remnants of the demon; both pieces were already blackening and shriveling into themselves. *One of the things I love is they clean up after themselves.*

I nodded to myself and smiled. Things were as they should be, or at least we were moving in the right direction. My mother's rotting corpse had been destroyed so no one could ever use it again, and the demon who'd committed the crime against her had been ended. Sure, the whole scenario was unnerving, and plain old disgusting, but I wasn't going to dwell. Not with demon children on the loose.

I still had a job to complete, and all the changes in my life to get a grip on. *But I'll be fine because I'm a unicorn, and making lemonade out of lemons is what we do.*

Chapter 22

"**N**othing!" I growled, slamming my fist against the wall. "How is it possible that he left nothing behind?"

Shuffling through a stack of papers, Bryn rolled his eyes. "What did you expect to find, a diary explicitly outlining everything he did?"

I flopped into the oversized desk chair, blowing an aqua piece of hair out of my face. "It would have been helpful." I toed the edge of the area rug. "I don't know, maybe I watch too much TV where everything works out in a timely and convenient way for the heroes." Kicking back, I surveyed the masculine office. Everything was oversized, and done in rich, earthy tones. I could understand why the demon had taken up residence in the senator's house. It had just the right amount of luxury without being over the top.

But who doesn't have books in their office? Maybe the

senator was too stupid to live? I slapped my hand over my mouth, even though I hadn't said anything out loud, shocked at my own nasty thoughts. No one deserved to die, even if they weren't an avid reader. It wasn't my place to decide who deserved to live or die, because if I did that would make me a monster.

Curling into myself, I wrapped my arms around my middle. I didn't know where all my hostility for a senator I couldn't even remember his name was coming from. Even though I had no lost love for politicians, some of the rottenest humans on the Earth, I wouldn't wish death on anyone.

My fists clenched, a dark ball of energy churning in my gut. *This isn't right. Something's wrong.* My heart set off at a gallop as adrenaline surged through my system. I was sensing … Sweat collected on my brow, dripping down my temples. I was sensing … "Bryn," I choked out. "Do you feel something … wrong?"

He lifted his gaze to mine, his eyes glowing. "Yeah, anger. I feel …"

Maddie stumbled into the room, grimacing. "I feel it, too." She slumped against the wall, her breathing ragged. "What is it?"

Standing, I gathered my magic, sending it outward, searching and assessing. Like radar picking up on a foreign object, something pinged in my awareness, drawing me out of the office. "It's this way, whatever it is," I murmured, knowing Bryn and Maddie would follow.

Goose bumps sprung up across my flesh, and my teeth

chattered, even as sweat continued to ooze from my pores. On wobbly legs, I shuffled down through the living room, down through the basement, and down another set of wooden stairs before I halted, unable to go any farther.

"What is it?" Maddie whispered from behind me.

Before us lay a hole in the Earth, or rather a gaping hole of … nothing. An absence of anything at all. And I knew exactly what it was. "It's a gateway to Hell."

Bryn stepped up beside me, pulling me into his arms as I shivered violently. "Is there a way to close it?"

"No, or at least not without catastrophic consequences."

"What do you mean?" Maddie demanded. "If there's a way to open it, there's a way to close it."

I shook my head, and squeezed my eyes shut. "Hell isn't an actual place like most think. It's a void, an absence of things. Which is why demons crave to destroy what we have here, and yet they covet it at the same time."

"If it's a void, then how do demon's exist at all?" Bryn asked against the top of my head, his lips warm. "And why is this … this nothing causing us to all feel so … wrong? I mean, isn't nothing something?"

"Demons are the only creatures who can exist in the void because they are empty themselves. Which is the reason they can only mimic emotions like laughter and happiness. But honestly, not a lot about Hell is known for obvious reasons. Anyone who enters is never seen again. It's suspected that the void isn't a true void by definition, or not all encompassing, and that it only sucks positive emotions, leaving nothing but hate, anger, and all the things that define a demon. It could be that demons were once exactly like us, before they stumbled into the dark."

Digging my nails into Bryn's shoulders, I bit my tongue as my teeth continued to chatter. The energy filled the air with the kind of chill that was an absence of heat, as if heat never existed. "It's stealing from us right now. Taking everything from us except the negative. But we can't close it. I can bind it, and conceal it, make it so no one is tempted to go looking for it."

Bryn shuffled us back a few steps. "Is it new? This gateway? Or has it been here the whole time?"

"Hard to say. But it's obvious someone went digging for it. The gate could have been here since the house was built, deep underground, or it could have sprung up for some unknown reason, like too much dark energy triggering it." That possibility was the most probable, and it made me wonder what kind of things happened in the outwardly beautiful home. It took an insane amount of negativity to cause a gate to Hell to spring up. Was the senator dead? And what about the rest of his family, aside from his daughter which I knew was possessed? The demon didn't necessarily have to have come through this particular gate, and instead could have been the one to cause or find it.

Stroking a hand through my hair, Bryn ground out, "I can't be here anymore. It's making me feel violent."

I pulled away from him, glancing back at Maddie who had fallen silent. Her gaze was riveted to the gate, her nails drawn into long claws. I swallowed around the lump in my throat. As much as I rejoiced at having Bryn and Maddie at my side, there were just some things unicorns had to do alone, and this was one of them. "Get Maddie out of here. Neither of you can handle being so close to a gate for very long. You'll both go feral. That's why it got worse when we entered the house." And it was what probably drove me to make my first ever demon kill. I'd been teetering on the edge with anger, the negative energy had simply given me a little shove without me realizing it.

"What about you?" Bryn ground out, scales rippling down his arms.

I smiled tightly. "I have enough positive energy to spare. At least enough to last me until I can take care of this thing."

Bryn ran his hands through his hair, flicking his gaze to the gate and back to me. "I can't just leave you."

Shoving at him, I screamed, "You have to."

"I thought we were partners, and now you just want to toss me aside? Do things on your own?" His voice vibrated with anger and hurt, his fists clenching and unclenching.

"You'll understand when you're not under the influence of the gate. Please, Bryn, trust me."

He shook his head, his lips curling back from his teeth. "How can I trust you when you don't trust me? Like what you did with the magic in the pancakes? I thought we were past that."

A knot of fury bubbled up in my gut, but I managed to push it aside. "We are past it. We're *Anam Caras* now. Use that, use our bond to feel the truth." Closing my eyes, I pushed my emotions at him, letting him know that I didn't want him to leave, but he had to regardless.

I snapped my eyes open in time to see him sift to Maddie, and both of them disappear. I heaved a sigh of relief. *It worked.* Bryn and Maddie were safe, and I could concentrate fully on the task at hand without having to worry about them.

Dropping to my knees, I convulsed, the negative energy pulsing all around me. *You can do this. You will do this.* Daegus had instructed me over and over about what to do with a gate, pounding the information into my brain until it became rote.

I imaged his stern voice laying out the steps.

"First you must immediately shift to your other form. All magical shifters are stronger in their nonhuman form, especially unicorns. You won't be able to fight the pull of the gate if you don't shift, remember that."

Duh. How could I have forgotten? What I'd told Bryn was true about me being able to withstand the dark energy from the gate, whereas he and Maddie couldn't, but not unless I shifted all the way.

With a burst of magic, I shook off the tatters of my clothes, and whipped my aqua mane and tale back and forth, expelling the negative energy that was trying to cling to me. Stomping one of my hooves, I stretched out my wings languidly. It had been some time since I shifted from my human state to unicorn, and I immediately regretted that decision. Just like any other shifter, I was as much human as I was unicorn, but I preferred my human form since I didn't have to hide it away. Although there was something ... freeing about being in my unicorn form.

"Step two," Daegus' voice rang out inside my head. "Remember the flight pattern I showed you? You must do it directly over the gate. The larger the gate the longer it will take you, but you must be precise."

Leaping into the air, I flexed my wings, diving to the right. I circled the void several times, before crisscrossing to make several x's in the air. It wasn't just about flying in a specific pattern, not anyone could yield the results I could from the aerial gymnastic I was performing. I was also trailing a ward spell behind me, and coming from a unicorn it was the most powerful magical binding in any known world. It was one of the many reasons we'd been hunted down since the beginning of time.

"Now focus, Talia," Daegus' voice commanded. "I know you, and once you get up there flying in fanciful patterns, you'll get distracted like you always do, but don't. You can only do the final step when you feel the air change, and for that you must be paying very special attention."

I chuckled to myself. Daegus had been spot on, I was a millisecond away from completely zoning out, my mind already wandering. I shook my head, and blew hot air out my nostrils. *Oh, that was the sign! The air will heat! I almost missed it!*

Diving down, I dipped my glowing horn into the center of the void, and counted to three. Pressure furled around me, like ghostly fingers yanking on my horn, pulling. The void was fighting back, resisting its inevitable fate.

Snorting, and baring my teeth, while my wings flapped furiously, I drew the final glyph, sending a blast of rainbow magic spiraling into the abyss. *You're no match for me!* A pop sounded, and an unseen force tossed me back. My body slammed into the dirt wall, crumpling to the ground.

Lifting my head, my eyelids fluttered as I watched the gate's energy still, as if frozen. *I did it. I put it into stasis. Go me! Now I just have to—*

Pain spiked into the back of my skull, washing away everything.

Chapter 23

Several pairs of red eyes glowed, weaving in and out of the darkness. Groaning, I attempted to stand, but couldn't. Chains rattled, chafing at all four of my ankles, and I quickly realized I was tethered to the ground, still in my unicorn form. My heart thrashed against my ribcage as panic set in, my nostrils flaring as they filled with the scent of earth and decay.

Calm down and breathe. Use your magic to get free. Unicorns aren't known for their brute strength.

Light burst into existence, causing spots to dance in front of my eyes. I blinked my surroundings into focus. *Damn it.* I was in a cage, and chained to the dirt ground, about ten feet from the thankfully still inactive Hell gate. *At least I got that part right.* The telltale red glow around the bars of my prison let me know I wasn't going to be making as easy an escape as I'd planned. *Double damn.*

Several demons, wearing the bodies of Girl Scouts,

milled around the space, as if they were unsure of what to do. "Um, hello? How about letting me out of here so we can have a little chat?"

Both girls scurried over to stand in front of the bars, their tiny hands reaching out to clutch the metal. The acrid scent of burning flesh met my nose, but neither of them flinched. *Okay, that's not normal, even for demons. They feel the pain their host body does.*

The girl with long, blonde hair spoke. "I didn't know unicorns had the ability of speech in both forms." She elbowed her companion, who merely grinned, her braces glinting red from the magic encasing my cell.

I sighed. "Unicorns can do a lot of things … so you better let me out before you piss me off."

"Nope. Our master told us to capture and contain you so that's what we did," the second girl said, sniffling indignantly.

Oh, you've got to be kidding me. Another weird thing. Usually the minion demons would automatically sense the demise of the head honcho, but not this time apparently. It was both a good and bad thing, if my predicament was any indication. I was also left unsure if I should inform them about the current situation. What if they headed off to get into mischief, before releasing me?

"RU!" Bryn sifted in behind the girls, wielding his dragon blade.

"Don't hurt them!" I yelled. "I don't want the bodies damaged."

He gritted his teeth. "So what am I supposed to do? The possessions are your expertise, not mine."

"Well, I can't exactly do anything from inside a spelled cage, now can I?"

The blonde girl lunged at Bryn with a low growl. He blinked out, and then back in a few feet away. "At least you got the gate shut down," he muttered. "I was about to lose it before."

"I still need to surround it with the magical deterrent so no one comes looking for it. Like I said, it's not closed, so it could reopen if the right demon knew what it was doing, or enough negative energy was fed to it. We need to keep it isolated." Which would do a whole lot more good when there weren't dozens of demons who already knew where it was. Thankfully they didn't seem to be powerful enough to counteract my wards to reactivate the gate.

"How do I get you out of there?" Bryn popped in and out of existence several more times, the demon girls running after him like two rabid dogs.

Maddie thundered down the stairs, putting her hands on her hips when she reached the bottom. "I told you to take me with you, Neanderthal. I had ride a wave all the way over here."

"I didn't have time to worry about you," Bryn snapped. "I'm her *Anam Cara*, and her guardian. What are you again?"

Her ebony skin transformed to cover her in armor. "A seriously pissed off mermaid who's going to make you pay

... after we get Talia out of here." She glided over to my cell, eyeing me with appreciation. "I gotta say, sweetie, you're absolutely stunning. I've never seen a unicorn up close and personal before."

"Tell me how beautiful I am later. Get me out of here now."

The blonde Girl Scout leapt onto Maddie's back, raking razor sharp claws across her chest. Maddie screamed with rage, and swung around, swiping her own claws at the tiny girl.

"No! Stop! Don't hurt her! She's possessed, remember? Just get me out and I can take care of the problem." I tugged on my chains and stomped my hooves. *At least hopefully this time I'll be able to.*

Maddie threw the girl across the room, and dashed for my cell. I was relieved when I saw her armor intact, and no wounds evident. "Too bad your magic didn't work on them back at the house. Would have made things a whole lot simpler," she huffed out.

I rolled my eyes. "Yes, because I chose to have my magic not work. Good times for everyone. At least we didn't need my magic to off the head demon since he came in his true form."

Both Girl Scouts froze, and then slowly turned to me. The blonde one said, "Master's dead?" She tilted her head, meeting her companion's red eyes. "Do you think she lies?"

The one with dread locks shook her head. "No. That

would explain why he's nowhere to be found even after we captured her."

An evil grin twisted blondie's lips up. "We're free!" They locked arms, and sped up the stairs.

"Shit," I muttered. "Why can't I ever keep my mouth shut?"

"Should I go after them?" Bryn asked, indecision warring in his blue, glowing gaze. He wanted to be with me, but he also had his duty to worry about.

"Yes, grab them for me!" I stomped my foot with impatience. *Now he waits for directions?*

Bryn sifted away, and back a few moments later. "They're gone. It's like they disappeared into thin air."

Fabulous. Two of the untrackable demons disappeared. That won't create any extra problems for us. "Just get me out of here." Sweat trickled down my face. The containment spell was cloying and hot, draining me of my power. It was as if thousands of fire ants were crawling across my skin, and I needed to be free soon or I was going to get seriously cranky.

Sifting to the door of the cell, Bryn ripped it away, breaking the magic containing me against my will. He rushed to me, managing to get the chains off in seconds, even though his hands were clumsy as they trembled.

As soon as they clattered to the ground, I shifted to my human form, launching myself into his arms. Whether it was the *Anam Cara* bond, or merely the stress of the day catching up to me, there wasn't a single place in the entire universe I would rather have been.

He peppered my face with kisses, covering almost every inch, as if he hadn't seen me in years. "Leaving you here unprotected, and then sensing your fear, only to find you in chains ..." He growled into my neck, the sound all dragon. "Never again."

I couldn't help but protest. I understood where he was coming from, I did. But he still needed to understand that as a unicorn there were going to be things I had to do on my own, whether he liked it or not. "Except for the whole getting knocked out and waking up in a spelled cage, I did fine on my own."

His fingers moved gently over my scalp, assessing. "You've got to stop letting people sneak up behind you and knock you out."

"Yes, because I do so enjoy getting my skull bludgeoned. Good times." Despite our dispute, our bodies were no less happy than normal to see each other. I pressed my mouth to his neck, drawing the sensitive skin between my lips. He groaned in approval, sliding his hands down to fondle my ass ... my still very naked ass.

"Guys, come on," Maddie whined. "We have so much to do, and I don't have time to wait around for you two if I want to make my date tonight. And I do think it's worth mentioning that my date is a very sexy dark fae I've had my eye on for quite some time." The sound of her claws drumming against metal met my ears. "Oh, and Excalibur is back in the lake for when you want him. In case you were worried he was lost."

I made a grunt of appreciation, not breaking contact with Bryn.

Maddie sighed heavily, her footsteps demonstrative as she made her way up the stairs.

Reaching into Bryn's pants, I cupped his rock hard erection. "I need you now, Bryn, please. Right now."

He fisted my hair, walking us towards the closest wall. "Do you think it's a good idea to be doing this so close to the gate?"

He dropped me to my feet and spun me around. "The more positive energy the better," I rasped. "And I can't think of any more positive energy than this. Can you?"

"Nope," he rumbled, sliding his hands along my hips to tip my ass up. "Can't think of one single thing."

Grabbing my wrists, he held them over my head as he pushed into me. Moaning, my head fell against the wall as I arched up onto my tiptoes. I'd only just met Bryn, our *Anam Cara* bond was fresh and new, but he was fast becoming a necessary part of my life. One that I couldn't imagine living without. My heart faltered, twisting into a knot.

And that terrified the shit out of me.

Shoving off the wall, I moved away from him, breaking contact between us. I spun around, my body still flushed with need for him, my pulse beating erratically, and his taste lingering on my lips. "Bryn, we can't. We can't do this."

His chest still heaving, confusion washed over him.

"What are you talking about? I thought you said this was a good idea, to put the positive energy around the—"

"Not that," I snapped. "This." I waved my hand between the two of us. "We need to find a way to break our bond. We can't be so wrapped up in each other. It's not good. It'll get in the way of … everything. Look how it is already, how fast we got to this point. Imagine months, years, and decades from now."

"No, you don't mean that. What's already between us is special. It's— I love you," he blurted, his expression stark. "I know you'll think it's too soon, or that I'm fooling myself into thinking lust is more than it really is, but I do … I love you, Talia White. So you see, you have to give us a chance, a real one, that's all I'm asking."

I let his words wash over me, spreading joy throughout every molecule in my body. I'd never had someone genuinely love me before—or not be *in* love with me. It lifted my spirit like nothing else could. But I knew the feeling couldn't last. I wouldn't let it.

"I'm sorry, Bryn, I don't … it's not the same for me."

His gaze clouded over, confusion swimming through his glowing eyes. "But I thought—"

"No. I love you … but as a friend. My best friend. Even that's soon when you think about it." The lie thickened the air between us, making it difficult to breathe.

Before he could react, I turned, stumbling towards the stairs, knowing if I stayed the truth would somehow leak from my pores, exposing me for the coward I was.

I love you, Bryn O'Bannon, more than I ever thought I could love anyone or anything. It doesn't matter how long I've known you, time doesn't matter when two souls connect the way ours did. We are soul mates. I know it for sure now. I've always known deep down, from the instant I first looked into your eyes and saw what lay beneath. I'll finally stop denying it. I love you so much it makes me physically ache. And that terrifies me— more than words could ever express. But you can never know. Never. Or you'll make it impossible for me to push you away. And I must. I must keep my distance. It's essential for my survival. If I lose you ...

I sprinted up the steps naked, not caring about any of it. All I knew was that I needed to put as much physical distance between us as possible. *Yes, I'm a coward. A coward because I'm afraid if I'm ever truly happy with Bryn, and I lose him ... I won't be able to go on.*

And then what? Then what?

Swiping at the river of tears running down my face, I steeled my resolve.

Yes, it's better this way. For the both of us.

Chapter 24

Bryn grabbed my arm, spinning me to him. With a grunt, my face smashed into his rock hard chest. He cupped the back of my head, holding me firmly in place.

"I'm sorry, I wasn't thinking. It's just …" A low growl rumbled in his throat. "I want you so damn much. And it's selfish. I know that. So selfish. I can let you go … if that's what you want." A fine tremor ran though him, belying his true feelings. He didn't want to let me go any more than I truly wanted to let him go. But that was the problem. I was afraid of what it would mean if I eventually lost him. Terrified, in fact.

"RU, please, I'm sorry. I took from you— I simply took advantage." His voice vibrated with anger. "You can't be so open and giving with yourself in this world. It's naïve of you to think so."

Did he seriously just chastise me for being open to him? I mean ... is he for real with this shit? The raw absurdity of it shifted something in me, reminding me of a few things. Things I could hardly believe I'd forgotten or ignored. Fear was not something I let run my life. Fear was a human motivator, an emotion that always bred hate in the end. If I let fear rule me, it eventually would ruin me, and steal from me the optimism that defined my attitude towards life.

My mood buoyed, changing my mind about everything. *Damn, I've been wishy-washy lately. I need to change that. Bryn is here to stay. He's my soul mate, something I've always dreamed of finding, and yet ever since he showed up I've been running scared.* Clicking my tongue, I rolled my eyes even though he couldn't see. "Don't be ridiculous. You couldn't be more wrong, Bryn O'Bannon. As usual. I'm not naïve. I'm the furthest thing from naïve. I, of all creatures, am well aware of all the horrible things lurking around almost every corner. I see it up here," I tapped my temple, "when I connect with demons." I paused for a moment, gathering my thoughts. What I knew was part of the problem. I was terrified of some of that darkness seeping into my life.

Swallowing hard, I continued. "It takes more strength than you can imagine to not buckle under the darkness in the world, to not let it snuff out my light, despite the fact that I'm a unicorn. Being the only lit candle in a pitch black room, well, the darkness pushes in around me. Surrounds me, threatens to eat me alive. It would be easier to let go, but I can't. It's not in me to do that. If I can guide just one soul, to help one person find their way from my illumination ... well, that's not naïvety, it's courage to stand alone against all odds." And that had been my problem lately, I'd been buckling under the pressure, letting myself get swept away in all the negativity. Letting fear drive me away from things I desired. *But I'm back now, bitches! Fear will not shape my life.*

"I don't want anyone to dim that light of yours. I—" He tangled his hands in my hair, pressing his chin to the top of my head. "I don't know what I'd do if someone hurt you. Changed who you are. Broke you. Especially if it was me."

I pulled away from him, meeting his tormented baby blues. "I'm not going to break. Not ever. And If I get hurt, I'll simply dust myself off and keep going just like I always have. I won't let this world, and all of the horrible things in it change me. I'll change it, make it better, inch by inch while crawling on my knees if I have to." I may not be a badass warrior, but I'm a badass in my own right. I'm a badass optimist who will never stop pulling myself to my feet.

Bryn's eyes lit up, throwing shadows across his face. "You're not like anyone I've ever known before."

"'Course not, silly. I'm a unicorn, and I'm pretty sure I'm the only one you've ever met."

"It wouldn't matter. I'm sure you're special even among your kind."

A lump formed in my throat. "I'd like to think my parents would be proud." I buried the image of my mother's zombified corpse deep inside the recesses of my mind, before it could resurface, hoping to never see it again.

Bryn reached out, ruffling my hair. "They would be. I know I am."

"What? You're proud of me all of a sudden? Just a moment ago you were trying to tell me—"

"A moment ago I was being a fool. I've seen the error of my ways now."

Yeah, me too. Me too, Bryn. Finally. I smiled. "Good. See. One more individual guided through the—"

His arm snaked out suddenly, pulling me back to him. He cupped the sides of my face in his huge hands, his dimples firmly in place as he gazed down at me with intensity. "So you want to remain *Anam Caras*? Is that what I'm hearing?"

I quirked an eyebrow and tilted my head. "You felt all of my emotions, didn't you? You knew when I wanted out because I was running scared, and you knew the instant I changed my mind back." I sucked in a sharp breath. "And you knew when I didn't tell you that I love you— Oh! You knew without me having to say a word." My cheeks heated, embarrassment washing over me. How could I fool him about anything ever? Not that I was planning on having tons of secrets, but what if I wanted to throw him a surprise party for his birthday or something? *Ugh. You wanted someone to know you completely, through and through. Be careful what you wish for, Talia. Be very friggin' careful.*

"Yeah. I sensed all of it." He swept his thumbs over my

cheeks. "Love is complicated enough without me deciding not to use all the advantages I have."

"And you were still going to let me go even though you knew I loved you?"

"Sometimes love isn't enough," he breathed, his lips scant inches from mine.

"It will be this time."

I had to believe our new love would grow into something wonderful, otherwise what was the point of soul mates? What was the point in anything at all, really? Love was a beautiful, positive thing, and if a besotted unicorn couldn't make it work with an infatuated dragon when they were soul mates, then who could? Sure, maybe our fledgling relationship had sparked from lust and the soul mate connection, and been sealed with a magical bond, but others have started with worse …

Arching into him, I smashed my lips to his, clutching his hard body to mine. We had some unfinished business to attend to, and I was already dressed for the occasion … or undressed as the case may be.

Bryn hefted me up, and I wrapped my legs around his waist. Moving backwards, he stumbled. Grinning against his skin, I took the opportunity to flip him on his back … quite literally. I shoved at his chest, using his moment of being unbalanced and my weight to take him to the ground.

The air whooshed out of his lungs at the point of impact, and I threw my head back with laughter. Dazed, he stared up at me, a slight quirk to his mouth. "What was that for?" he croaked.

"A girl likes to be on top sometimes." Without breaking eye contact, I reached down to undo his pants. "Didn't think you'd mind."

He smirked. "No complaints here, but maybe a warning next time would be nice."

I pressed my finger to his mouth. "Shhh ... I have to concentrate." Licking my finger, he bit down gently.

As soon as I freed his cock from its prison, I impaled myself, letting out a long moan. Leaning forward, I braced myself on his chest, and used my knees as leverage as I began a blistering pace. His hands flew to my hips, his fingers digging into my flesh as I rode him hard.

Mmm ... yes. Ride 'em cowgirl. I internally sniggered.

With every downward stroke my clit rubbed against him, and with the combination of that and penetration ...

"Yes, oh fuck, yes!" I screamed, my body clenching around his as I faltered and swayed.

Taking over, Bryn slammed into me from below, grinding rapidly as he spasmed inside of me. "Fuck," he growled.

Collapsing over him, I tucked my head against his chest. "I needed that."

"Yeah, me too." He slid his hands down my spine, settling them on my ass.

"Yep, sometimes a girl needs a quickie on the floor of a house where there's an inactive Hell gate in the sub-basement to get her going. And also sometimes she needs to feel like a romance heroine who has sex at wildly inappropriate times. It was all quite thrilling. Good job." I patted his shoulder.

Bryn chuckled. "I feel used."

"You should. I'm only in this relationship or bond or whatever because you're hot, and you know how to use that beautiful cock of yours in all the right ways."

He nipped my ear. "I can live with being used by you every day if necessary."

"You better be able to live with it because unicorns like me have needs. Needs that you'll be expected to fulfill without complaint."

"I would never complain."

"Mmm …" Smacking his chest, I stood, glaring down at him with mock annoyance. "Now come on, lazy dragon-boy, we have demons to track down, get off of the damn floor."

He jumped to his feet, bowing low before me, while peeking up through a swath of midnight locks. "As you wish."

I rolled my eyes. "You are not Wesley."

"No, I'm better."

I rolled my eyes again more demonstratively. "Whatever. Let's go. I'm serious now." Turning, I swung my hips as I padded across the floor.

Bryn grabbed me from behind, sifting us back to my bedroom. "You need clothes first. Can't let you walk around naked, you're a unicorn not a mermaid."

I snickered. "You have a point." I paused on my way to

the closet. "Hey. Did you leave Maddie back at the senator's house?" She had definitely made herself scarce while Bryn and I had been working out some of our issues.

Bryn shrugged. "She can take care of herself."

I raised my eyebrows, and crossed my arms over my chest. "Bryn," I chastised.

"Fine. I'll go look for her while you get dressed." Sifting away, he left me alone.

Warily, I cracked my closet door open, half expecting a demon child to jump out at me. As far as I could tell the wards to keep unwanted guests out were still up, but after having them banging on my front door I was a bit paranoid.

Note to self: Double check the wards, and after this mess is all over, put some kind of hiding spell on the house as well. I'd find a way to stay in my home. There was no way I was letting a bunch of demons chase me away. *Nope. No way, no how.*

Chapter 25

"How do you plan on tracking down all of the demon spawns?" Maddie glanced up from her nails briefly, before she went back to applying a second coat of ruby red nail polish. She was lounging on my bed, getting ready for yet another date, while Bryn and I attempted to put together a decent plan.

"You still can't sense them, like with other demons?" Bryn asked, a disdainful expression directed at Maddie. He hadn't wanted her around ... big surprise. But the two of them were just going to have to learn to play nice since they were both card-carrying members of Team Unicorn Talia, even though neither of them wanted to wear the shirt.

I flopped back on my bed, nibbling on my thumbnail. "Nope, still can't sense them and I don't have a clue why. I've never run across demons that I couldn't immediately sense from miles away. Those little buggers can be holding my hand and I get nothing. Zilch. Nada. And I have no idea why. And let's not forget about my magic not working on them. This whole thing is beyond anything I've ever dealt with before." My lower lip stuck out in a pout against my will. I couldn't seem to help it. I was over this hunt, and ready to move on to other things. Like taking care of the non-possessed children in my area. They were probably all skin and bones without my weekly gifts of baked goods to their families.

Unicorns had a way of becoming attached to their places of dwelling, having the need to coddle and protect its residents. It's where the lore of unicorns and their magical forests had begun ... because it was more than lore, it was the truth. Except now in the twenty-first century modern unicorns preferred houses with hot water to roughing it in the wilderness. At least this one did.

Wait. Children. Food. Hmm ... An idea percolated in my brain, bringing a smile to my face. "I know!" I jumped up, clapping my hands together. "I'm going to make cupcakes! Lots and lots of cupcakes!"

Bryn's eyebrows shot up. "Not that I don't love your cooking, but really? Cooking is your solution to the demon problem in Tennessee?"

"Don't underestimate the power of cupcakes, especially when made by a unicorn." Skipping out of my room, I was already designing the perfect mix in my head. My secret ingredient being my demon banishing magic, of course.

Bryn traipsed after me, scratching his chin. "What are you up to? I can sense you scheming."

Bounding down the stairs, I glanced back at him, smiling innocently. "Unicorns don't scheme, it's not in our nature."

"Yeah, and if I believe that one …" He lifted his brow in vivid skepticism.

"Whatever, you'll see." I flounced into the kitchen, and set to work.

THROWING MY HEAD BACK, I cackled. *Oh, this is going to work wonderfully. My magic not doing the job before could have been because the minions have some kind of protective spell … but this time I'll hit them from the inside.*

"I thought only witches cackled?" Bryn muttered, not looking up from his dragon blade. It gleamed and glinted, winking at me as he polished it at the kitchen table.

"One of my ancestors was probably a witch."

"One of your ancestors was definitely a dragon," he replied. "It would explain a lot."

Huh. That *would* explain a lot about how easily our magic intertwined to form the *Anam Cara* bond. But I didn't have time to think about any of that now. *Focus. The end of this hunt is nigh!* I cackled again.

"Laterz, Talia, sweetie." Maddie glided through the kitchen, her long, purple hair cascading in perfect ringlets down her back, her skin shimmering with glitter, and her makeup done in purples and blues, all of it complementing her iridescent cocktail dress just right. Even her nails matched. *Guess she decided not to go with the red after all.* "I have a—"

"Date, yes we know." Bryn lifted up his blade to study it, wiping a cloth down its length. "When don't you have a date, and where do you find all these willing sacrifices?"

Maddie shimmied in her dress, motioning to her body. "Most males would do anything for a mere chance at a piece of this."

Bryn's gaze roved her body from head to toe, before he turned back to his work. "Guess I'm not most males."

Maddie clicked her tongue. "You're a mated dragon, of course you aren't interested in anyone but Talia."

"I wasn't interested in you before I was mated," he retorted.

"You already had a thing for her," she snapped. "I bet it was devotion at first sight. Poor dragon didn't have a chance." She patted him on the head on her way out the door.

He growled under his breath, baring his teeth as she pulled the lock shut.

"Oh, just ignore her. I think she likes needling you. I have to admit it's pure fun to get you to react so easily."

Bryn sifted behind me, wrapping his arms around my waist, his hands resting on my stomach. "You definitely get a reaction out of me easily." He pivoted his hips against my ass, showing me exactly how much of a reaction.

Mmm ... mama could use her own specially made Bryn

dessert. Wait. What? Ugh. I swatted at his shoulder. "No time for that now." Lifting one of the finished cupcakes, I turned it so he could get a good look. "What do you think of my masterpieces?"

Resting his chin on my shoulder, he studied my work. "It seems like a normal cupcake to me, if all cupcakes resembled unicorns that is."

Bryn was right. The design wasn't anything that hadn't been done before. Heck, there were pages and pages devoted to clever unicorn cupcake and cake designs on *Pinterest.* Mine simply had a little something extra that the naked eye couldn't spot: my magic. Within the rainbow icing that curved into manes, around the tiny ridges winding up the golden horns, and even in the fluttery eyelashes on the front of the cups, was a spell especially designed to yank nasty little demons out of their unwilling hosts. With a big nasty, like the one I'd already laid waste to, the cupcake wouldn't work, but with weak minions who didn't even blip on my radar ... easy peasy. At least I hoped. *No. It'll definitely work because it's the perfect plan. It'll bypass any outward protection spell ... and voila`, death by cupcake.* I cackled yet again.

Setting the cupcake back down on the counter, I turned in Bryn's arms, fingering his hair at the nape of his neck. He shivered, leaning into my touch. "That's the beauty of it. Because it's so blatantly a unicorn, they'll never suspect it's a trap laid by a unicorn. It's kind of like hiding the plan in plain sight."

"So what's the spell in the cupcakes supposed to do

exactly? And why do you think this will work when your magic has been on the fritz?" Bryn skimmed his molten lips down my neck, eliciting a pleased shiver of my own from me.

"I suspect my exorcisms haven't worked because of some kind of unknown protection spell. The cupcakes are like a Trojan horse, slipping in to attack from the inside. Once they take a bite the magic will purge the human children of their unwanted guest, leaving a delightful sugary aftertaste for their trouble." Plus, I'd put an astronomical amount of magic into each cupcake. If they didn't work, I was officially retiring. After all, how was a unicorn supposed to do her job if her magic couldn't take care of a few minor demons?

"But where will the demons go?"

I frowned. "They really didn't focus on your education much at all, did they? You should know this stuff."

Nibbling on my shoulder, Bryn smirked against my flesh. "How do you know I'm uneducated and I'm not simply making sure you know what you're doing?"

"Not likely."

He chuckled against my skin, nipping again. "Yeah, not likely." His fingers skimmed up my waist, and over my nipples, teasing briefly before falling away. "What can I say? When I was just a wee dragon, when I was supposed to be learning my lessons, all I could concentrate on was the physical part of my training."

"You are quite talented at the physical stuff." I bit my lower lip.

Moving back to the table, he folded his huge body into the chair, picking up his dragon blade again. "I'll stop distracting you so you can finish baking your dastardly little treats. We'll have plenty of time for ... the physical stuff when we finally finish this hunt."

Focusing back on my masterpieces, I added the sugary horns to several more of the cupcakes, humming "Hit Me with Your Best Shot". Somehow it seemed appropriate. "Turn on the news, would you? I want to see if any of those kids made it back on there."

Flicking the ancient set on, the TV flickered before the picture settled into a somewhat discernible scene. "Guess we'll never know exactly what happened with those disappearing kids, huh? Aside from the fact that they all showed back up with demons in tow."

My timer dinged, and I bent over to remove another pan of cupcakes from the oven. "That's the thing about real life, we don't always get the answers we want, although in the end it doesn't matter in this case."

"Suppose not," Bryn mumbled, smacking the TV to bring the picture back into focus. "You need a new TV, this one is crap."

"It's really old, and I don't want a big monstrosity in my kitchen. That's what the living room is for, which is actually how that piece of junk ended up in here. Daegus swore he wouldn't buy a TV for the kitchen, and he didn't. That one was free. He totally loopholed me."

"... *have gone crazy. Dozens of children, ages thought to range from seven to fourteen are roaming the streets of downtown Nashville causing chaos." The camera panned down lower Broadway, showing several police cars smoking and on fire, children dancing around laughing and screaming. "The authorities have been unable to contain them, nor have they discovered who their parents are. The mystery of ..."*

Bryn flicked the TV off. "You better bake faster. Seems like you were right about them turning into gremlins without supervision."

"I can only go so fast." I grimaced, icing a row of cupcakes haphazardly. "If they don't look good enough to eat, then they won't, you know, eat."

"Hope Nashville is still standing by the time you're ready." Pacing over to hover next to me, he asked, "Can I help? I've never actually," he motioned to the cupcakes, "well, any of it. But I can try."

I patted his arm, smearing icing on it. "I appreciate the offer, but if I don't make them then my magic won't infuse them with the spell like I need."

Bryn brought his arm up to his lips, sucking his tongue back into his mouth before he could lick the icing off. "Umm ... this won't do something funky to me if I taste it, will it?"

"Like what?" I whisked more batter, glancing over at him.

"I don't know, like freeze my face into a painful smile for hours."

"Stop giving me a hard time about the pancakes. We both know you have that convenient little glyph on your chest to protect you from such things now." I sighed heavily, pouting. "You're never going to let the pancake incident go, are you?"

"Maybe in about ten to twenty years." He chuckled. "No, I take that back. I'm never letting it go."

"I changed my mind. You can help by going away," I snapped.

"I can sense that you really aren't mad. You just want me to think you are so I'll stop distracting you."

Pouring batter into the cupcake tins, I ground my teeth. "This *Anam Cara* thing is going to take some getting used to." I'd been trying to block Bryn out, keep him from sensing every tiny emotion. It was kind of unfair since he seemed to have a better handle on it than I did. Of course he was used to channeling and using dragon magic, to me it was a new and foreign skill, and would take a bit of getting used to.

"You love it." He kissed my forehead, swatted my ass, and promptly sifted away.

I smiled to myself. I kind of did … love it that was, knowing we were a forgone conclusion and not a guessing game. *Soul mates, destined to be together, bonded as Anam Caras.*

Okay, focus. Cupcakes, cupcakes, cupcakes. Then Bryn.

Sighing, I got lost in images of naked Bryn as I baked my little heart out.

Chapter 26

"**I**'m done!" I yelled, slumping against the edge of the counter.

Spread out on every available surface in the kitchen were hundreds of adorably enchanted unicorn cupcakes. It had only taken me most of the day and night.

"Good." Bryn strode into the kitchen. "Because I've been keeping track of our little gremlins, and things are insane downtown." He ran his hand through his hair, his expression pensive. "I know they're demons, but they're still in the form of children. Who would have thought they could do so much damage?"

"They have a knack for destruction, and because of the bodies they're inhabiting it makes it difficult for people to know what to do." Untying my apron, I dusted flour from my dress. "Now we just have to get my cupcakes to the demonic rugrats, and all our problems will be solved." *Hopefully.*

Bryn scratched the scruff on his jaw. "How are we going to do that without them seeing us?"

"I have a plan. A real one this time."

Opening the back door, I whistled. Hundreds of woodland animals scurried into view, situating themselves across my back porch, awaiting for what I was going to say. Crouching down, I flitted my gaze over everyone from the possums to deer. The whole crew was in attendance. I idly wondered if anyone had stayed behind, or if the forest would be suspiciously empty until the job was done. It was a bit crowded at the moment.

"Now, this is very important, so listen carefully." My furry friends remained silent and attentive, their eyes trained on me. "We need to protect our world from demons by getting them to eat some cupcakes I magically spelled. You can't eat them, understand? You have to get them to the demons. They're not for you. If you eat them then I can't save out world, and nobody wants that."

As I continued to give instructions, Bryn lugged trays of cupcakes outside, setting them on the patio where there was space.

"Just make sure they don't see you. Leave them in places that would seem natural, like humans were having a party or something and were scared off before they could eat."

A flurry of animal sounds met my ears, letting me know they got it, and were on board.

"I still don't understand how we're going to get all

these cupcakes downtown to where the demons are," Bryn eyed the waiting animals, "at least in one piece."

I turned to him, batting my eyelashes. "Did I forget to mention that my favorite beastly creature was going to be flying everyone downtown?"

"Favorite beastly creature?" His shoulders slumped when it finally clicked. "Oh, come on. You expect me to fly all of them on my back? What about the humans? It would be easier to sift them."

"You can't sift them, the enchantment in the cupcakes is really fragile, and I don't know how your magic with interfere. And like you're the first dragon to be spotted by humans. You know they always rationalize stuff like you away."

Bryn sighed heavily. "It's different in these times with cell phones, and everyone ready to record things at a moment's notice."

"It's getting dark. You're a black dragon. No one will see you."

"You don't have a back up plan, do you?"

"No." I smiled sweetly. "Do you?"

"Guess I'm flying everyone to downtown Nashville on my back."

Walking into the clearing by the woods, he started peeling his clothes off. Despite the situation, I was riveted, my breath catching in my throat as his pale skin was exposed to the chilly evening air, piece by piece. I leaned against the deck's railing, fighting the urge to fan myself.

Bryn was magnificent, and no matter how many times I'd seen him naked, I wasn't sure I'd ever tire of the sight.

His eyes met mine, his irises lighting up, just before he threw his head back, and a wave of magic permeated the air. A moment later, instead of Bryn in his human form, in his place crouched a gigantic black dragon.

I crept across the lawn, drawn to explore his new form. I was fascinated by this dazzling creature who was my soul mate and *Anam Cara* as sure as I was his. Steamy air puffed out of his nostrils as I laid my hand on his long snout. His eyes, although larger, were the same, highlighting the soul of the male I'd come to love so quickly.

"You're beautiful," I murmured, moving down his flank, trailing my fingertips along his scales. His entire body was covered in them; dark, gleaming scales. Black in color, and yet appearing iridescent where the light glinted just right.

Bryn made a chuffing noise, digging his claws into the grass as his tail flicked back and forth. He somehow managed to sound impatient and annoyed, despite his lack of words. I patted his haunches. "Yeah, yeah, I'm almost done. I can't help but be curious about you in your dragon form."

He snorted, puffing steam from his nostrils, a low grumble shaking his body. "Yeah, whatever," I snapped. I wasn't exactly sure what he was inferring, but I didn't like his tone. *I really need to figure out how to read his emotions through our bond. It would make my life so much easier.*

Circling him, I stopped to touch his wings. They were so much different than mine. A unicorn's wings, at least those lucky enough to be born with them, were made of feathers, much like a bird's in appearance, but softer, and somehow sturdier. But Bryn's wings were like a bat's, made up of bone and leather-like skin.

Magic swirled through the air, and Bryn stood in front of me in his human form again. He scowled down at me, his arms crossed over his muscular chest. "As much as I'd love for you to fawn over me all day, I prefer my adoration to be without the added pressure of worrying about demons destroying an entire city while it's happening." His forehead crinkled as he studied me. "How did Daegus keep you focused for longer than five minutes?"

Swallowing to return moisture to my throat, I forced my gaze up from … some of his more interesting parts. "If you don't want me distracted then maybe you shouldn't stand in front of me buck naked. There's a suggestion. Plus, I thought you told me it was harder to change forms for you than other dragons. So don't waste your magic on my account."

Bryn growled. "I only shifted back because I can't speak mind to mind like most dragons."

Leaning over, I bit his ass. Hard. "Change back now or I won't be responsible for what happens next."

His eyebrows lifted to almost his hairline. "That's supposed to be a threat? Sounds to me like you're trying to drag me down with you into distraction land."

"Drag you down with me? Please. You get distracted just as easily as I do."

"News flash," Bryn crowded my personal space, "no one gets distracted as easily as you do."

"Ha! That's a lie and you know it!"

"You're doing it right now," he growled. "You're so caught up in convincing me how you're not easily distracted," he raised his arms up in the air, "boom, you've completely forgotten about the animals behind you waiting to complete the job you tasked them with. And if I let you we'd probably ..." He snapped his jaw shut, transforming back to his dragon form.

Smacking at his snout, I leaned into his gigantic face, glaring. "You change back right now, Bryn O'Bannon, and tell me what you were going to say." He shook his head, his tail twitching. "I mean it! Change back right now!"

Maddie poked her head out from around a large tree. "Would you two keep your bickering down, puh-leeaze. Some of us are trying to do important things and need to concentrate."

"Didn't you have a date?" *Wait. Was that this morning? Or last night? Or yesterday?* I'd officially lost track of time. "Or did you bring him back with you?" I waggled my eyebrows.

Maddie snickered. "Geez, I hate to agree, but Bryn is right. You really do get distracted easily."

"Do not." Except I was well aware of my adeptness for losing focus at the drop of a pin. I simply didn't like admitting my shortcomings out loud, or to anyone but myself.

Maddie rolled her eyes. "Whatever." She disappeared back into the woods, leaving me with a gigantic, impatient dragon.

"Change back, Bryn."

His eyebrows shot up, which were nothing more than ridged scales above his eyes. I was pretty sure he was in disbelief how I latched onto certain things, like wanting him to change back to tell me what he was going to say, and forgot others, like ...

"Shit. The cupcakes." Scurrying across the lawn to the deck, I checked my tiny masterpieces over, making sure they weren't melting or getting attacked by insects. I flicked at a large directionally challenged moth, hoping I didn't injure it in the process. Unfortunately, I held no sway over insects such as them, although bees did seem to dig me. *Focus, Talia. Don't let Bryn be right ... again.*

I clapped my hands together. "All right. Let's do this."

Chapter 27

Glowering at me, Bryn sank deeper into my massive tub. "This stuff better work," he grumbled.

"I said I knew how to fix you, and I do." I upended another can of tomato paste over his head, biting the insides of my cheeks to keep from laughing. In actuality, I merely needed to say a minor incantation to cure Bryn of his Eau du Skunk. But the way he'd stomped into the house hemming and hawing about what a catastrophe my plan had been … well, I kind of wanted to punish him a bit. Besides, the outcome of my plan hadn't been revealed yet. The animals with my sugary exorcism delivery systems had been shuttled downtown via Bryn, but I hadn't wanted them to stick around in case things went awry. So to say it was a failure already was completely uncalled for.

"You didn't have to include skunks in your little plan. I

hit a bit of turbulence, one little pocket of air, and the lot of them started spraying everyone."

Turning the can opener, I pried the lid off another can of tomato paste. "At least it was on the way back, and not when you still had the cupcakes. That would have been a disaster."

Cupping some of the paste in his huge hands, he splashed it over his chest. "Yes, *that* would have been what made it a disaster."

Adjusting the cotton balls in my nose, I dumped more paste over his head, red gook bouncing off of him to splatter on my floor. Sure my bathroom was a disaster area, and I had to deal with Bryn's current state of stench longer than I had to, but ... *totally worth it.* I was also tickled pink that he somehow hadn't picked up on my lie. Although I was pretty sure it was because I was dancing around the truth, lying without actually lying. It was a trick I'd picked up from the fae, tricky little buggers that they were.

"How long do I have to sit in this crap before it works?" Bryn crinkled his nose, sniffing his arm for the umpteenth time.

Seeing him sitting there, the massive dragon warrior that he was, covered in tomato paste from head to toe ... I couldn't take it anymore. I burst out laughing, doubling over to clutch my stomach. "Not too much longer," I hiccupped out. "Not much longer at all."

Bryn stood, the paste sluicing down his body, sticking in some very interesting places. "I don't need to be doing this at all, do I?" He cursed under his breath. "I should have known. I felt something off, but not completely. You tricked me."

"I do know how to get the skunk smell off of you, but I'm a unicorn ..." More laughter erupted up my esophagus, causing me to sputter. "I don't need tomato paste like a human."

"You lied without lying. I didn't know you had it in you."

"I'm a fast learner, and you made it completely worth my while to put into practice that little fae trick."

"It won't work again. Now I know what I was sensing."

I smirked. "I'll figure something else out then."

"To hell you will." Sifting out of the tub, he grabbed me around the waist, saturating my dress with tomato, and yep, the glorious scent of skunk perfume. Despite the cotton balls, I choked and sputtered, my eyes burning.

Clawing at his forearms, I squealed, "Stop it! You're ruining another dress!"

He buried his face in my hair, rumbling against my skin, "Maybe you should have thought of that before you started covering me in tomato."

Squirming in his unbreakable embrace, I kicked at his shins. "You deserved it for being such a cranky asshat, and you know it. You insulted my plan, and we don't even know if it worked or not."

He reached around and deftly plucked the cotton balls from my nose. The immediate overwhelming stench wound its way up my nostrils and down my throat. I doubled over, retching. "Let me go, Bryn. I'm gonna puke."

"Then make it go away. Fix it now because I know you can."

Covering my nose and mouth with my hand, I sagged in his arms. "Fine." I quickly said the necessary words under my breath, instantly nullifying the smell.

Releasing me, Bryn waltzed over to the shower, dripping red clumps all over my floor. *It doesn't feel like it was worth it anymore. Cake not worth the bake.* After all, I was the one who was going to have to clean up the mess. *I need to find a cleaning spell, or track down a cleaning fairy or something.*

I nibbled my thumbnail, staring at Bryn's perfectly formed rear end as he climbed into the shower. "Bryn?" I shuffled forward, suddenly ashamed of myself. Maybe he was behaving immature, but as always, two wrongs don't make a right. He was trying, legitimately trying, and I was being spiteful because he'd inadvertently hurt my feelings. I could have explained that to him, but instead I'd made the choice to punish him. What kind of relationship could we hope to build if I constantly acted like a brat?

"Yeah, what is it?" He turned to stare at me through the glass, water cascading over his head.

"What if it's always like this between us? What if we can't ever stop bickering over ... everything?"

"Then things will never be boring between us, that's for sure." He poured a generous amount of shampoo into his hands, working it into a lather before rubbing it into his hair.

"I'm serious. What if we can't stop fighting?" My heart dropped into my stomach. I would never be able to live with the constant tension. The last few days had been one thing, but I generally preferred tranquility to drama. I wasn't one of those beings who enjoyed constant chaos. When I imagined a future with Bryn, I wanted it to be with us on equal footing. With us understanding each other on a soul deep level. Not with me having to battle him to gain a single inch on any significant issue. I loved reading romance novels with the Alpha males and females, and their unrelenting battle for who was on top, but none of that was me. Frankly, it sounded plain exhausting. Fantasy was a fantasy for a reason, and although I would always be an optimist, I was also a realist. I wanted a mature adult for a partner, not a belligerent dragon, no matter how incredibly sexy he was. Nor did I expect him to settle for a brat of a unicorn.

Finishing up with one last rinse, Bryn switched off the shower, and grabbed my towel from the hook. Never taking his gaze from mine, he quickly dried himself off, and then sauntered over to me.

"Come here," he said, opening his arms wide.

Unable to resist, I threw myself at him, my cheek painfully smacking into his pec. "What are we going to do?"

He kissed the top of my head, smoothing his hands down my back. "For one, you're going to get out of this dress because I just showered and you're getting tomato all over me again."

Sniffling, I dug my fingernails into his lower back. "I'm serious. You know I don't mean right now. I mean in the future ... with our relationship."

Sighing, his breath ruffled my hair. "We're going to have growing pains. Lots of growing pains. But I think as long as we both try, as long as we agree to communicate better then we have a real shot at being happy."

"You think?"

"Where did the little optimist go?" he murmured, tilting my chin up with his knuckles.

"She's still in here." I gave him a shaky smile, the edges of my lips trembling.

"I won't let you down, RU, I swear it. I'll never give up, I'll do my best, and just like I told you before if my best isn't good enough ... I'll get better and try again."

"But—"

He brushed a soft kiss against my lips, shushing me.

"We're going to fight, about a lot of things because we're both strong willed and passionate, and used to doing things our own way. But as time goes on we'll work more and more things out. We'll find a place to coexist in peace together. We'll make it happen. It'll just take time."

Staring into his earnest eyes, I swore I could see his very soul. He was the male I wanted to be with, the male I would give my all and try my very best for, and if that wasn't good enough ... well, I was a unicorn, so it would definitely be good enough, at least eventually.

I ran my fingers along his jawline, needing to touch him. "How did this happen? How did we end up here so fast?" Despite the knowledge that he was my soul mate ... all of it seemed surreal somehow.

"Maybe it wasn't fast at all. Maybe we've both been preparing our entire lives for each other."

Which on some level would make sense since we were soul mates, but even still ... I guffawed. "I didn't know you had it in you to be so corny."

Pulling away from me, he scowled. "Way to break the moment."

Oops. There I went again, opening my mouth when I shouldn't. "I'm sorry, Bryn." I invaded his space, wrapping my arms around his neck.

He shrugged me off, not meeting my gaze. I internally cringed. Bryn was sensitive. It'd taken me all this time to actually realize it, which was utterly ridiculous. It was as obvious as the sky was blue. He was a dragon warrior, sure, but he was also a male with the need to be open, to have an intimate emotional connection. He'd chosen me for that honor, and yet every time he attempted to open up, I scoffed at his emotions. *Stupid, stupid, stupid unicorn.* I was being just as much of an asshat as he'd ever been, maybe worse since I was supposed to be better at empathy ... being a unicorn and all.

Wrapping my arms around Bryn's waist, I pressed my face into his chest again. "I'm sorry, please, I'm sorry, sorry, sorry. I can't say it enough how sorry I am. I didn't mean to marginalize your feelings. I didn't—"

"I'm not a chick," he rumbled, moving to push me away.

I only clung to him tighter. "Don't do that. Don't hide your feelings from me because I was dumb enough to laugh at their authenticity. I think … I think it's because I don't want to admit to myself how much I love it when you say that sappy shit to me. I love it, and I'm afraid to love it because then one day what if I lose it? Then what? What would I do then? I think that's why I'm having trouble reading your feelings through our bond because I have a mental block built up on fear. I'm afraid of losing you. So I'm still pushing you away even though I promised myself I wouldn't." I sucked in a lungful of air, having blurted all of that out without taking a breath. And it rang with truth. I'd claimed I wasn't going to let fear hold me back, and yet I'd simply been letting it hold be back in a completely different way than before.

Bryn's arms tightened around me. "We'll work it out. You and me together, we'll figure it all out. We just need time."

"You know how you keep saying I'm nothing like you expected a unicorn to be?" I smiled into his skin, barely resisting the urge to bite his nipple. "Well, you're nothing like any dragon warrior I've ever met before. But in a good way." He was gruff, and had the tendency to default to factory dragon asshat settings, but underneath it all, Bryn was exactly what I wanted and needed. "And I don't want you to hold back your feelings because of me. Of course I make no promises that I can withhold any snark.

It's who I am, and even though I support and love your mushy dragon innards, that doesn't mean if you lob a slow pitch at me that I—"

Lifting me off my feet, Bryn spun me around, setting me on the sink. "Are you done?" He quirked an eyebrow, his pupils dilating as his irises sparked with light.

I nodded, reaching for him. With the press of my mouth, the slide of my tongue, and each caress of his skin, I'd show him exactly how I felt ... no words needed.

Chapter 28

"Nothing on the news yet?" I paced back and forth across my living room, nibbling on my nails. "If my cupcakes worked then don't you think there'd be something on the news about it? At least a five second clip. Something."

Bryn kicked his feet up on the coffee table, and stretched his arms across the back of my couch. "Give it time. It's only been a few hours. Maybe they weren't hungry yet?"

"Please, they're demons in the bodies of children. They're hungry." What if something went wrong? What if my magic still wasn't working? Or what if the minions weren't as stupid as I'd thought? *But isn't that the prerequisite to being a minion of any kind? Lack of brainpower? Otherwise they'd be the actual villains.*

"Sit down. You're making me nervous."

I threw my hands up in the air, glaring at the ceiling. "I can't sit because I'm already nervous."

"You want to go down there to check on things?" he asked nonchalantly.

"Yes! That's the dumbest question ever! Of course I want to go down there!" Why hadn't I considered that an option before? "We can fly down to Nashville together." My lips curled up as I pictured us flying side by side, him in his dragon form, and me in my unicorn form. I sighed with delight.

"You can wipe that sappy smile off your face because I know what you're thinking and it's not safe. We can't fly together like you want. But I can take you down there on my back if you're set on flying instead of sifting."

I flopped onto the couch, curling into myself. I knew he was right. Daegus never let me fly around in my unicorn form either since it was too much of a risk, the consequences staggering if I was to get spotted. And yeah, Bryn couldn't technically order me not to do something like Daegus could, but it was time for me to be act like an adult. Just because I was only thirty years old, practically a baby in the supernatural world—Hell, I wouldn't even come into the majority of my powers until I was half a century old—didn't mean I could continue to act like a child when it came to impulse control. Look where that had gotten me so far. Not that I could complain about having Bryn as an *Anam Cara*, I'd lucked out with him, but it could have all ended in disaster.

Bryn snapped his fingers in front of my face. "Hello in there? Where'd you go?"

"Just thinking about how much it sucks to be an adult," I harrumphed.

"I don't know. I can think of a few fun things for adults only," he slid his hand up my inner thigh slowly, "and none of those things suck."

I smacked at his hand playfully. "Yeah, yeah, sex is great. But what about the rest?"

"Tell you what? After this hunt is done and over with I'll take you to my clan's land so you can fly without having to worry about being seen."

"Really? Daegus never let me do that. He said I had to learn to live without that joy because of—"

"And I say differently." He tugged me into his lap, cradling me against his chest. "Daegus had to raise you, and because of that you became like a daughter to him. But I'm your *Anam Cara* and I want to do everything in my power to make you happy."

"I want you to be happy, too. I don't want to cause trouble for you."

"Shhh …" He brushed his full lips against mine. "I'll be happy if you are. It's how it works for a male dragon in an *Anam Cara* bond."

"That doesn't seem fair. We should be equally happy." I wasn't sure I fully understood how the whole *Anam Cara* thing worked between us, especially because it wasn't a normal bond, my unique magic making it a bit wonky, but

I did know I wanted Bryn to get just as much satisfaction on all levels as I would.

"We will be, I promise." He nipped at my lower lip, his hands cupping my ass. "And I'll be exceptionally happy if you get naked with me right now."

"Bryn," I chastised. "We need to go check on the demons."

"I have to get naked anyhow in order to shift into a dragon. We might as well enjoy it a bit first." He waggled his eyebrows, grinning wickedly.

I groaned. "As much as I would love to ... well, you know, right now. We need to put an end to this case once and for all. We can't have it hanging over our heads for all of time."

Sighing, Bryn said, "You do have a point. Not one I'm particularly liking at the moment, but both of us have been—"

"Focused on all the wrong things since you got here. Yeah, I agree."

"They're not wrong." Bryn strode to the kitchen, glancing back at me with raised brows. I scurried after him. "We've just been shit at prioritizing."

He was right. Dealing with our relationship dynamic when he'd first arrived had been the number one issue to focus on since we couldn't go on a hunt if we were literally at each other's throats. But after we were relatively settled, our partnership and bond shouldn't have continued to top the list of important things. Neither of us was going anywhere so there'd be plenty of time for relationship drama. We were both behaving like adolescents in love for the first time.

Hmm ... or maybe that's part of the problem. Neither one of us has ever been in love before and we've both been acting the fools.

Shaking my head, I trailed after Bryn into the backyard, my body crying out for me to change my mind and take him up on his offer. "So this is what being an adult is like? Told you ... it sucks."

Bryn stripped his clothes off quickly, shifting into his dragon form as soon as he was naked. Smart, because I wouldn't have been able to keep my hands off of him in my current mood.

Gathering his jeans and T-shirt, I hopped onto his back with ease. "Giddy up!" I rocked forward, digging my heels into the sides of his long neck. He snorted, his tail flicking up with agitation. "Oh, come on. I've never actually gone for a ride on a dragon's back before. If Daegus had to transport me he'd carry me in his talons."

Searching for a place to grip so I wouldn't fall off, I wiggled back and forth, sliding right off his back. He made a chortling sound, his scaly eyebrows going up in question. "How the hell did all those animals stay on without seatbelts?" My eyes widened. "You didn't lose any, did you?" He shook his head as he rolled his eyes. "Then how did they stay up there?"

His form shimmered, and naked Bryn replaced the dragon. "Wild animals are obviously more adept at surviving on a dragon."

It was my turn to roll my eyes. "Please. There simply isn't anywhere for me to hold on. You're not telling me how they stayed up there." I waved my hand at the empty space he'd occupied in dragon form.

"Look, I honestly don't know. But clearly it seems like I'm going to have to carry you like Daegus did. Either that or we change our transportation method and sift."

I had my heart set on flying. If I couldn't do it as a unicorn, I at least wanted to get up there in the air. "Maybe I could fashion you a little saddle?"

He crossed his arms. "Nope. I'm not wearing a saddle. Besides, where would it go when I shifted back to human?"

"Couldn't you just make it go wherever you make your dragon blade go when you're not using it?"

"No, it doesn't work that way. Our swords are magically spelled to wait in the in between. We can't send whatever we feel like there."

"Why not?"

His face contorted with disbelief. "I don't know, we just can't."

"But did you ever actually ask if you could? And if they said no—whoever you asked, the dragon elders or whatever—did you ask why? I mean, is there limited space? It just doesn't make sense." I narrowed my eyes at him. "Or did you do that dragon thing where you accepted it was what it was, tradition or what not, and didn't bother finding anything out?"

"I-I, well …" he sputtered.

I pursed my lips. "That's what I thought. You need to ask more questions, Bryn. I bet you could send whatever you want off to *Never Never Land*."

He ran his hands through his hair, making it stick up at odd angles. "You make my head hurt sometimes, you know that?"

I scrunched my nose up. "Not the first dragon to tell me that. Must be a genetic issue."

"Enough," he growled. "I'll just carry you in my talons. No saddle."

"Oh, but a saddle would be so cute. I could get a purple one with gold inlay. And maybe sparkles. Or—"

"We don't have time for any of this now. No saddle," he growled, shifting back to his dragon form.

I stuck my tongue out at him. "Party pooper." *Yep, I'm well on my way to being a mature adult.*

Sitting up on his haunches, Bryn turned his front leg over, and opened up his talons. I climbed in, settling myself cross-legged in the center of his ... hand ... paw ... dragon grabby thingy? *Whatever.*

Although I'd flown with Daegus the same exact way dozens of times, it felt different with Bryn. New and exciting, like we were setting off on a grand adventure. I sniggered, pointing out through his two front claws, and exclaimed, "Allons-y!"

He huffed out a breath, rising slowly up into the air. Once we'd cleared the trees, he dove forward, the wind whipping my hair back. My nose and ears chilled almost instantly, burning, and my breath was visible with each excited puff.

The night sky zoomed by, lights glittering beneath us. And before I knew it we were circling the Batman building in downtown Nashville, our journey ending too soon. A few flaps of his wings later we were landing behind the old train station off of Tenth.

Sliding out from between Bryn's talons, I jumped the few feet to the ground, landing with my skirt above my waist. As I hastened to adjust it, Bryn shifted, snatching his clothes from under my left arm.

"Is this where you landed before with the animals? It's a bit of a trek to get down to lower Broadway."

"It's only a few blocks," Bryn responded through his shirt as he tugged it over his head.

Yeah, a few dozen blocks. "You don't think anyone saw us?" I scanned the windows above us, all of them appearing to be dark and empty.

"The news reported the hotel and beer emporium were closing until things downtown were taken care of."

"Makes sense."

Taking my hand within his, Bryn led me across the deserted parking lot, his bare feet giving me cause for concern. I'd forgotten to grab his shoes before we'd left. He didn't seem to be bothered by it though.

"Maybe you should pop back and get your shoes. Wouldn't want to step on a needle or glass or something?"

Bryn smirked. "I'm a dragon, none of that will really hurt me. Plus, you can heal me if I do."

"If I feel like it," I retorted, pulling my hand out from his. I wanted him to get shoes so I didn't have to worry about him, but no, he had to be an asshat and throw my words at me from eons ago—okay, a few days—at me.

"All right." He dipped down to kiss me on the forehead. "If it makes you feel better I'll get my shoes."

He disappeared, leaving me alone in what felt like an apocalyptic wasteland. *Me and my bright ideas.* Dashing up the ramp, I climbed into the empty train, hiding out of sight until he got back.

"Hurry up, Bryn. How long does it take to find shoes, anyways?" I nibbled on my nails, crouching in the dark.

Come on. You face off with demons all the time, but standing in an empty parking lot creeps you out? What do you think is going to happen? An army of clowns is going to appear out of nowhere to devour your soul? I shuddered, wrapping my arms around my middle. *Hurry up, Bryn! Hurry the frig up!*

Chapter 29

"What are you doing in here?" Bryn scanned the interior of the rusted out train. "Did you think you saw a clown or something?" His lips compressed with the obvious effort not to laugh.

Now that was a hell of a coincidence. Or was it? "Hey! Not fair. You sensed I was thinking about clowns through our bond."

His eyes widened. "No shit? You actually got spooked because you were thinking about clowns? I was joking."

"Lucky guess." Pushing past him, I stalked out into the chilly night air. "It's awfully quiet around here. Suspiciously so."

"And that conjured images of clowns?"

"Shut it, Bryn, or I'll borrow a car and drive us home."

He ground his teeth together as he took my hand within his, tugging me after him. "Let's just go check on the demons, or hopefully lack thereof in downtown Nashville."

He was right ... again. *He's getting seriously annoying with that shit.* I'd allowed myself to get distracted by my overactive imagination ... again. "Can you give me a piggyback ride?"

"What? No."

"But I thought you wanted me to be happy." I stuck my lower lip out in an exaggerated pout. "It would make me happy not to have to walk all the way downtown in my cute, but seriously uncomfortable shoes." Glancing down at said shoes, I bent over to dust off invisible dirt. They were blue suede booties, which matched my red and blue dress perfectly.

"You're just being lazy and you know it."

I shook my head. "No, I'm not. I didn't think through my shoe choice before we left." Lifting up my right leg, I pointed at my foot. "These need broken in before I go for a hike in them."

"So you'll break them in on this ... hike."

"Bryn," I whined. "Please." He scooped me up in his arms, cradling me to his chest. "I don't want to be carried like a baby." I smacked at his chest. "I just wanted a piggy back ride."

"Non walking beggars can't be choosers," Bryn said, his dimples popping out. "I'll carry you how I want." Clomping down the sidewalk, he stared straight ahead, concentrating on our surroundings.

I pressed my nose into his neck, inhaling. "You smell so good," I purred.

"Stop that. I need to pay attention so we don't get attacked."

"Sorry," I muttered, not sorry at all. With the silence permeating the night air, I wasn't worried about someone or something getting the jump on us. I was becoming increasingly sure my cupcake plan would be dubbed a success.

"Shit." Adjusting me in his arms, Bryn sifted us behind a brick building, and dropped me to my feet.

My heart sped up, and I was instantly on alert. "What is it?" I whispered. "What did you see?"

He leaned into me, his hot breath fanning across my ear. "A couple Girl Scouts."

"Doesn't mean they're demon Girl Scouts." He raised his eyebrows. "Fine. They're demons. I can't believe my plan didn't work." Bryn opened his mouth, and I pinched his lips together. "I don't want to hear an 'I told you so' from you, Mr. O'Bannon."

He backed away, raising his arms. "Wouldn't dream of it." But his smug smirk said it on his behalf.

"We need to spy on them. See what they're up to and figure out what went wrong."

"Let me guess, you have another plan?"

Flipping my hair over my shoulder, I grinned. "Of course I do. Sift us down to the river."

"And then what?"

"And then we spy on the demons, duh."

His right eye twitched. "Daegus planned all the strategy for when you were tracking, didn't he?"

I tilted my head. "Yeah, so? What's your point? He would have messed this all up, too. We never had a situation like this before. My magic has never not worked. Sue me for not being fully prepared for having a power outage." Latching onto his arm, I bounced up on the heels of my feet. "Now, come on, sift away."

"This is going to end badly," he grumbled.

I smacked his shoulder. "Take that back, you're going to jinx us."

Ignoring my comment, he grimaced, and then sifted us.

Appearing on the grassy bank of the Cumberland, I hit the ground instantly. We couldn't afford to be seen. "Get down!" I tugged at Bryn's pant leg, hearing a tear.

Standing over me, Bryn crossed his arms. "Yeah, because that'll make us invisible."

"Just get down," I hissed.

Unfazed, he strode up the sloped hill, scanning the area. "There's no one around."

Scrambling to my feet, I dashed after him, peeking around his massive frame. "Where are they and what are they up to?"

"Maybe those Girl Scouts I spotted are the only ones left?" he suggested.

"We better check." Sprinting past him, I headed for the corner of the closest building, paying no mind to what it was. I peered around him and registered much of the same—empty streets, and no one in sight. "Come on." Making a run for Broadway, my new shoes dug into my heels, and rubbed on the sides of my feet, causing me to wince. I paused, tilting my head to listen, before rounding the corner of the next building.

A squeak escaped my chest, and I skidded to a stop, frozen with surprise. The silence had been misleading. There, sitting on the pavement, in the middle of the street were what appeared to be all of the demon children.

The Girl Scout with long blonde hair locked eyes with me. "You," she said. "I guess we should thank you for our delicious treats."

It was then I noticed the cupcake papers strewn around them, littering the street. "You ate them?"

"Every single one," another girl with short, dark hair responded, licking her fingers for effect.

And yet here they all still were. What went wrong? Was the spell not strong enough, or did it—

But it had to be. I'd used up everything I had. Why wasn't my magic working on them? I was at an utter loss. *Maybe it really is time to retire.*

The blonde girl took a few steps towards me, and I backed up, hitting Bryn's firm chest. "I can tell by the confused expression on your face that you can't understand how we're still here after eating your spelled treats."

"That thought might have crossed my mind," I said, eyeing the destruction all around us. Windows were broken, cars upended, and scorch marks ... everywhere. It was as if they'd tried to burn down everything, and got bored before they actually did it.

"We're not what you think we are," a little boy said.

"You're not demons?"

"Let's get out of here," Bryn whispered in my ear.

"No, not yet. I'm not going to just run away." His arms came around me, but he didn't sift us … yet. At least we were making progress, although I didn't think he'd wait much longer.

"Demons?" The little boy laughed. "What made you think we were demons?"

"I don't know, red eyes, and the fact that your demon master pretty much told me so. And all the rest …" I waved my hands at the destruction they'd left in their wake. "If it walks like a demon …" I put my hands on my hips, waiting.

"Well, we're not, demons," the blonde Girl Scout spat. "We're something else."

"And you're not going to tell me?"

"Why should we?" the little boy demanded. "So we can arm you with what you need to send us back to where we came from?"

Okay. Not as stupid as I'd thought. Probably the opposite. The more comfortable a creature is with playing dumb, usually the more intelligent they actually are. "It's why I couldn't sense you. It explains everything." At least I knew why my magic hadn't worked on any of them. It was kind of difficult to expel a demon when said creature wasn't an actual demon. *So what are they?*

The Girl Scout with dreads grinned, her braces glinting. "Ah, she's finally getting it. I thought unicorns would be more exceptional than you are."

"So what were you doing following a demon's orders then?"

The little boy stood, kicking an empty can. "He lured us into his service with the promise of getting to live in this world, and we entered into a bargain. But with him gone, we're free now."

"And we like this world," a brunette girl chimed in. "It's so much more fun than where we came from."

The little boy nodded. "Yes, we have power here. But not in our world. At least not enough."

I'd been compiling the pieces in my head, and they finally all fit. There was only one other creature the children could possibly be. "Changelings," I exclaimed. "All of you are changelings."

Silence fell, all of them staring at me. Their shocked expressions confirmed. Finally the little boy spoke. "Fine, you know what we are now. It won't save our human counterparts, or send us back to our world."

I tapped my chin, studying them. They were such good copies of human children, I would never have guessed what they were if they'd been determined to stay hidden. But they'd gotten greedy, and now I knew exactly what they were and what to do.

"You're right," I said. "I may not be able to send you home with my magic, or save the human children who you ripped from this world." I leaned more into Bryn, making sure we were touching. "But I know of someone who has that power."

"Who?" the blonde girl spat. "Tell us who!"

"Psst ... I'm not going to tell you."

"Ha! You're bluffing."

"Am I?" Turning to Bryn, I met his gaze. "Hold on tight to me."

His irises lit up, confusion washing across his features. "What?"

"I said to hold on tight." His arms wrapped around me, and I struggled to breathe.

Closing my eyes, I pictured the fae realm. It would be a bumpy ride, but I could get us there.

"RU, what are you—"

His words were ripped away as we were sucked through a portal I'd managed to conjure, but just barely.

Chapter 30

Sputtering, I spit grass and dirt from my mouth, the scent of fresh earth the only thing I could smell. "Bryn?" I clawed at the ground, attempting to find purchase. When I said it'd be a bumpy ride, I hadn't been kidding. I was pretty sure we'd made it through the portal, but I was left drained and disoriented.

"Here," he groaned from somewhere on my right.

Flopping over, I took in the view of purple sky with puffy blue clouds. The thing about the fae realm was that it rarely looked the same twice, except for the lands around the light and dark courts. I'd never actually traveled there myself, but I'd been warned countless times by Daegus about the dangers of leaving my birth realm as a unicorn. I'd still have my magic, but because I was out of my element I'd be weak until I acclimated. And even then, I'd never be as powerful as when I was at home, drawing energy from my land.

Bryn's face appeared above me, his features in shadow. "This is fairy?"

"Technically this realm is called Alternum, which means other, I think. Our realm is Mundi, which translates to mundane ... I think." I slicked Bryn's hair out of his eye while chewing on the inside of my cheek. "Witches and fae pay more attention to the names and protocol. I know just enough to get by."

"Get by? I don't like the sound of that."

"I never actually planned on coming here. Daegus only taught me survival tips in case I found myself here one day by accident. When I was about ten I opened up a portal when I was trying to conjure ice cream." I shrugged. "He thought we should be prepared in case I did something like that again."

"And now you came here purposefully? Great." He stood up, and offered me his hand. "Tell me about these changelings."

Sliding my hand into his, I let him pull me to my feet. "I'll tell you on the way."

"To where?"

I spun in a circle, searching for the clues Daegus had told me about years ago. "Aha!" I pointed in front of me. Off in the distance, the sky seemed to fade to royal blue, which meant that would be where the Light Court would be. I'd landed us relatively close. *Go me!* "This way." Locking my arm through Bryn's, I dragged him forward.

"Are you sure you know where you're going?" He dragged his feet, scanning our surroundings for danger.

"Of course. I wouldn't wander around Alternum without knowing where I'm going. That would be bad."

"Yes, very bad. So you're sure?"

"Yes," I snapped. "I remember Daegus telling me to head to the Light Court if I ever ended up here. And I also remember him telling me that the Light Court could be found under the royal blue sky." I motioned to the purple sky, and then waved at the blue sky in the distance. "See, we need to go over there."

"I could sift us. Wouldn't it be—"

"No. You don't know how this realm will affect your powers. It's best not to use any of them until you know. I don't want us to get separated."

"Fine. So tell me about these changelings, and why we're risking our lives to come here."

"I never said we were risking our lives."

"You didn't have to. Even I know to steer clear of this place and I didn't know what it was called. The fae are deadly, and their powers unpredictable."

"We won't be here too long." I smiled wanly, hoping he wasn't picking up on my nerves through our bond. Maybe I'd get lucky and Alternum would make it difficult for him to use the *Anam Cara* link temporarily.

Swiping at my brow, I gathered the sweat there. "But we had to come here, Bryn, otherwise dozens of human children could die. Plus, we can't let changelings run around our world to do whatever they want. You've seen the destruction they've already caused in such a short period of time. Imagine when they start to grow in size and power."

"I'm still not sure what changelings are," Bryn grunted, tucking my hair behind my ears without missing a step.

"Ever hear the old tales from Scotland and Ireland about the parents of newborn babies swearing that their child wasn't the same, that it'd been changed out with some other creature?"

"Please don't tell me those are true."

"Most stories are based in at least a little bit of truth." Stumbling, I clung to Bryn as he wrapped his arm around my waist, keeping me on my feet. *Stupid shoes.* I cleared my throat. "Changelings are fae shapeshifters who take on the form of a human to take their place. But they only get the one form. Once they choose they're stuck. The human then lives out the entirety of their lives here in Alternum. If you kill the changeling before the bond between the two is broken then the human child will die, too. The changeling draws its energy from its look-alike. It's all very complicated. Bottom line: we need to get the children back, and break the bond. "

"And they're powerful, the changelings?" Bryn scooped me up in his arms, and hopped over a weird tree thing, although I'm sure it was breathing.

"Powerful enough in our realm. Here not so much, which is why they enjoy going to live in a human's place. It's unusual for so many of them to be there together though. They usually like to stay inconspicuous. Especially since the ruling fae here in Alternum forbid them to steal human lives like in the olden days. It's too risky in modern times and everyone worries about exposure, even the fae."

"So your plan is to report the changelings to the Light Court and hope they fix the problem?"

"Exactly."

What I didn't tell him was that I'd ultimately be risking my exposure by going to the Light Court. Alternum had a way of revealing hidden faces, and lies. In the name of self-preservation I should have left the changelings alone since they were technically not my problem because they weren't demons, but ... but ... the children. I had to save the children, even if it meant exposing myself as a unicorn to hundreds of fae.

Bryn stared down at me with concern. "What aren't you telling me? I sense something ... off with you."

"I'm nervous is all." Turning my head, I studiously avoided his gaze.

"Don't bullshit me, RU. You're nervous because of whatever you're not telling me."

Damn, stupid Anam Cara bond. It's more trouble than it's worth sometimes. So much for it not working here. Plastering a fake smile on my face, I waved my hand. "Nah, you're being paranoid. It's this place, it messes with your mind."

He grabbed my arm, halting me in my tracks. "Why are you still trying to lie to me when you know I can sense—"

"As I live and breath, I never thought I'd run into you here, Talia."

My head whipped around, locking on the familiar

figure. I hadn't seen him since ... an unbidden memory sprung up.

"Daegus, no!" Clutching at my unbuttoned dress, I sprinted after my guardian. "Daegus, please, don't hurt him!"

But my dragon of a father figure wasn't listening as he crashed through the woods wielding a flaming sword, hell-bent on decapitating my very first lover.

I shook my head, dispelling the image. "Zan, is that really you?" There was no mistaking him though, my former fae lover was unforgettable. He hadn't changed one bit since the last time I'd seen him, nearly fifteen years ago. His skin was golden, shimmering as if he'd been dusted with fine glitter, offset by his pale blond hair that fell past his shoulders. Tall, almost as tall as Bryn, but not quite, he was lithe and muscular, his all white garb practically see-through.

I remembered my hands gliding over that smooth, golden skin as he pressed into me, his dazzling green eyes staring deep into mine as I gifted him with my virginity. Our time together had been limited, but nice ... until Daegus crashed our party of two.

Zan bowed deeply at his waist, a wicked grin spreading across his chiseled features. "Have you come looking for me, after all these years?"

I snorted. "Please. You ran away from Daegus like a terrified child. You didn't even attempt to defend our relationship. Nor did you attempt to seek me out after that. You ran and hid, telling everyone this side of the veil to steer clear of me."

Zan's features pinched with annoyance. "Who wouldn't run from a crazed fire dragon determined to kill them? And if I couldn't have you, I wanted no other fae to claim what I coveted."

"Oh, so on top of being a huge baby, you were selfish. Yep, you're just the prize I've been waiting for all these years."

Zan closed the short distance between us, and grabbed my hand. Dipping down to perch on one knee, he pressed his firm lips to my knuckles. "Please forgive me. I—"

Bryn yanked me away, and tucked me into his side. "That's about enough of that," he growled.

Zan stared at Bryn a moment, his green eyes narrowing. "Another dragon? And this one you … let him claim you?"

"That's none of your business, Zan," I snapped.

Bryn growled, his grip on me tightening. "Keep away from her and don't even think about trying to slobber all over her hand again."

"Why are you here then? If not for me?" Zan leaned back against a blood red tree, yawning in boredom.

Why did I ever like him again? Oh, right. Because he's smoking hot, and purely decedent with his kisses. "Why are you lurking around out here? What is it that fae do in their spare time?"

He pushed off the tree, circling us slowly. "Hmm … fae, something you are clearly not, do whatever amuses them because they can. I much prefer playing games of seduction wherever I can find it as opposed to causing mischief, buuut ... today seems different."

"What do you mean I'm not fae? I told you—"

"Your protection glamour was stripped the moment you stepped onto Light Court land. I finally see you for what you are ... unicorn."

I knew it could happen, and I thought I was mentally prepared, but a gasp still escaped my mouth at being called out. "I don't know what you're talking about."

Zan continued to circle us, his eyes roaming up and down my body with studious detachment. "I don't know how you ever fooled me to begin with—me, fae royalty. But you did. Somehow even when I was buried deep inside of you, your glamour held."

Spinning to face Zan, Bryn shoved me behind him, his dragon blade appearing in his right hand. "Don't speak about her like that or I'll finish the job Daegus couldn't manage."

Zan laughed. "Dragons, so territorial. And what about you, tall, dark, and pissed off, I suppose you have no past lovers? You were untouched until dear Talia found you?"

Peeking around Bryn, I watched as Zan ran a finger brazenly down Bryn's chest. "Most fae enjoy company of both sexes in the bedroom, in case you didn't know, and I certainly wouldn't mind a dragon, unicorn sandwich."

Jealously spiked, and I pushed around Bryn, shoving at Zan. "Hands off, asshat. He's mine, and I don't share."

Zan sighed. "Pity." His gaze hungrily traveled over the both of us, and he licked his lips provocatively. "Let me know if you ever change your mind. The invitation is always open."

"We won't," I snapped.

"So, my dear Talia, what brings a unicorn here to the Light Court? Tired of hiding yourself away and come to offer your services to our king?"

"No. We have a changeling problem in Nashville I need taken care of."

He tapped his chin. "Ah, I see. But did you really think coming here and exposing yourself was a good idea? You have to know that most here would kill to use your powers."

"And what about you? Would you kill to have access to my powers?"

Zan smiled. "As I've already stated, I prefer seduction to other methods, and I plan on having the both of you under my spell very soon. You could fare far worse as far as protection goes."

"She has all the protection she needs," Bryn snarled.

A fae guard—wearing shiny, silver-toned armor—appeared beside Zan, scowling down at him. "When your cousin sent you out here to fetch the unicorn, he didn't expect you to take all day."

Zan sighed heavily. "I also didn't know the unicorn would be someone I know." He winked at me. "Come on. My cousin, the king, is very interested in meeting you, Talia. But remember my offer, and consider it before his, since we do have history together."

I pressed into Bryn's side, nerves tightening my chest.

What have I done? Maybe I should have washed my hands of the changelings for self-preservation. *No. You have to save all those children.*

Things would work out somehow. I had to keep the faith. After all, being an optimist is about having hope, and seeing the light or even the possibility of it despite the darkness. Sure, things were grim now, but I had to believe good would come from my sacrifice.

Notching my chin up, I met Zan's gaze. "Lead the way. I'm interested in meeting your cousin, the king, as well."

Chapter 31

"Uncle Crel!" Dashing across the throne room, I jumped into the burly dragon's arms. He swung me around just like he'd done when I was a toddler, and he came to visit his much older brother, Daegus.

Setting me on my feet, Crel backed up a few steps, his expression sobering. "Why would you come to Alternum?" He stalked over to Bryn, invading his space. "Why would you let her come here, Bryn?"

That's right. Uncle Crel would know Bryn since Bryn was raised in the same clan. Of course my uncle was red dragon through and through, his short red hair bright against his pale complexion.

Bryn's lips curled back in a snarl. "As if I could stop her."

"Daegus would have."

Shoving the two of them apart, I stood with my hands

out. "Stop it. We had to come here, Uncle Crel. Bryn had no choice."

"There's always a choice," he growled.

"Now, now. No fighting in my throne room. Crel, darling, come sit by me while we talk to your niece. Your very unicorn niece who you've never once mentioned to me, by the way."

I turned, coming face-to-face with the King of the Light Court. He was tall, at least six foot four, but seemingly larger by way of presence. His platinum hair was intricately braided and pulled away from his strong, chiseled features, highlighting his rugged jawline, and pointed ears. Diamond eyes glittered, catching the light, as they flitted around, taking in both Bryn and me. His skin was flawless, and golden, baring a hefty resemblance to Zan, his lithe muscles encased in white leather enriched with silver lining, something I was pretty sure only someone like him could pull off. The King of the Light Court was what one would call savagely beautiful, and yet he was refined by fae elegance, a study in contrasts, just like all of his race.

He inclined his head, barely a nod. "I am King Anyon, ruler of the Light Court. And by your surprise at finding your uncle here, it seems as if my naughty *Anam Cara* has been keeping many secrets."

"*Anam Cara?*" Bryn and I said in unison.

King Anyon clicked his tongue while shaking his head slowly. "Crel, I thought you loved me."

Crel placed his hands on his hips, smirking. "I keep just as many secrets from you as you do me."

"Wait." I waved my arms around frantically. "Uncle Crel, you and the King of the Light Court are *Anam Caras*? How? When? Why?"

Bryn had been able to become my *Anam Cara* because of my unique magic, but I hadn't thought it possible with a dragon and a fae, let alone a male fae. Usually the bond could only be formed between two dragons, or if one was full-blooded and the other at least part dragon, a hybrid of sort, it was doable. There was also the little matter of a male dragon being magically able to control the bond. Female dragons had definitely pulled the short straw in the genetic lottery on that one. I wasn't even sure two male dragons could technically form an *Anam Cara* bond, since magic is linked to genetics not love. So how did it work with a male dragon and a male fae? It obviously had, but I was confused … by all of it.

Maybe I don't understand the whole Anam Cara thing as much as I thought. Or … my heart warmed at the sudden thought, *maybe dragon magic is evolving and changing, making it possible for love of all kinds to exist within the clans. Now wouldn't that be something?*

Zan, who had remained quiet until now, said, "Everyone knows, once you go fae—"

Bryn spun, grabbing Zan by his throat. "Not another word from you."

"Oh, dear." King Anyon placed his hand on Bryn's

shoulder. "I know my cousin is annoying, but please don't kill him, my aunty would be most agitated with me."

Bryn let go, and Zan crumpled to the floor, disappearing a moment later with a flick of King Anyon's wrist. "There, all better. We can talk civilly now, being that we're all family here."

"Zan was technically family," I blurted, "being that he's your cousin."

"He's from the dull part of the family. He doesn't count." Striding across the room, the king sprawled across a white leather chaise, kicking his feet up.

Figuring it was time to get to the point, I shuffled across the white marble floors, Bryn close at my back. "We have a changeling problem in Nashville."

Uncle Crel took up position beside the king, his body stiff as he glared at Bryn. "A changeling problem is not a reason to come here and expose yourself."

"I have to save the children!" My face crumpled, my cheeks heating. I was one millisecond away from bursting into tears, which would be utterly humiliating.

Uncle Crel's expression softened, and he sifted to me, pulling me into his arms. "Don't worry, Anyon will take care of everything."

"I will?" King Anyon's voice went up a couple of octaves. "But I have so many other things to do."

"And you'll help *my niece* first."

"But changelings are nothing more than a nuisance, they can't—"

Turning away from my uncle, I addressed the king.

"Maybe to fae, but they're more than a nuisance to humans."

He sighed, flipping his platinum hair over his shoulder. "I suppose I do often forget how powerless and fragile humans are." He grinned, flashing perfect teeth. "Or you could simply accept the position I was going to offer you in my court, and forget about the humans and their dull world."

"The children," I hissed. "We can't let the human children live here in this realm indefinitely."

"And why not?" King Anyon retorted. "If I brought them all here to live in the lap of luxury, what's the harm in that?"

Uncle Crel loomed over the king, his green eyes glowing with anger. "Help my niece. Help her save the children, and take care of the changelings." The king opened his mouth, but Uncle Crel cut him off. "And no, Talia is not going to be a part of this court. She has responsibilities in her own realm."

Bryn's arm snaked around my waist, and I leaned into him, accepting the comfort he was offering. "What about her exposure? Is there something to be done about that?" Bryn demanded. "Surely, the King of the Light Court can hide her presence from his subjects."

King Anyon stared at me, his diamond eyes glittering with some unknown emotion. "All of Alternum already knows of Talia and what she is. Her magic bloomed across this realm, announcing her to every creature big and small the moment she stepped through that portal. There is no going back into hiding for her."

Panic iced up my spine. "I'm sure that's not entirely true. Sure the fae know unicorns exist now, that we weren't all killed off eons ago, but I can move, put up more glamours, use—"

"My kind will never stop searching. Your power is something all will covet, but I'm sure you knew of the dangers when you came here."

I nodded. "Yes, I did. I just thought—" What? I thought I could get some kind of magical do-over? There was a reason why Bryn's clan had dedicated their resources to keeping me hidden. I gulped. For the first time in my existence, I was genuinely terrified of what my future would bring.

"King Anyon will find a way to protect you," Uncle Crel offered.

The king pinched the bridge of his nose. "Darling, as much as I love you, I'm finding it difficult not to throttle you right now."

Flames ran up Uncle Crel's arms. "You will find a way. You must."

The two shared a silent conversation, their eyes locked. A few moments later, King Anyon looked over to me. "He's right. I will find a way. Now go—go back to your life in Mundi, and continue on with whatever it was you were doing there."

Hope surged. "Really? I don't have to do anything else?"

"No," Uncle Crel ruffled my hair, "go home and continue as you were." He lifted his gaze to Bryn. "And if you put her in another position like this, I will kill you myself."

I jumped in front of Bryn as if I could shield him from my uncle's threat. "Be nice, Uncle Crel. After all, he is my *Anam Cara*."

"Which is the only reason why he's still alive."

"Oh, stop. You know he couldn't keep me from coming here, and you're crazy to think I'd let you touch one hair on his head."

King Anyon came to stand beside my uncle, throwing his arm around his shoulders. "Go now before I change my mind," he said.

Grabbing Bryn's arm, I tugged him after me. "We're going." I glanced back, waving with my free hand. "Bye, Uncle Crel, thanks for your help. Come visit me soon so we can catch up. And whatever you do, don't tell Daegus about any of this. Please!"

Uncle Crel waved back, but didn't say a word about Daegus. *Shit. He's going to spill. And I'm never going to hear the end of it. Shit-shit-shittity-shit.*

"Hold on tight to me, Bryn. This is going to be another bumpy ride."

I closed my eyes, and opened a portal home.

Epilogue

I bustled around the kitchen, singing a made up ditty about baking. It was nonsensical and weird, but I didn't care. I was happy. And when I was happy I baked. And when I baked I made up silly songs.

Bryn and I had arrived home to find things … normal. At least as normal as they could be since I was still a unicorn, and he was still a dragon. But the changelings were gone, and Nashville had already moved on, rationalizing the supposed children's crazy behavior on a gas leak of all things. *Really, humans? How many times are you going to fall for that lame-o excuse?*

I hadn't heard from Uncle Crel, or King Anyon, which I took as a good sign. *I still have so many questions there.* Nor had Daegus come bursting in to give us a proper talking to, and throttling Bryn within an inch of his life while he was at it. And last, but not least … No swarms of fae visitors had shown up either, announcing my presence to the world. *Yep, everything seems like it's back to normal.*

So I moved on, too. *Business as usual. Plus, the added bonus of a super sexy dragon of my very own.*

Opening the oven, I pulled a pan of chocolate chip cookies out. "Bryn, come and—"

He sifted in beside me, snagging several cookies off the pan before I could slide them onto the cooling rack. His cheeks puffed out as he chewed.

"You could at least wait until they're not like molten lava. You're going to burn your mouth."

He pointed at himself. "I can conjure fire. I don't think it's possible for food to burn me." He shoved several more cookies into his mouth.

I rolled my eyes. "Dragons."

The kitchen door slammed open, and Maddie sashayed in, wearing her usual attire of next to nothing, her gold string bikini leaving little to the imagination. "So, you ever going to train with Excalibur or are the two of you going to play house from now until eternity?"

"I'm getting there." I slapped Bryn's hands away from the un-iced cupcakes on the counter. "Not until they're done."

He eyed them with an exaggerated pout. "I bet they're good now."

I quirked an eyebrow. "And they'll be better when I'm done."

Maddie made a grab for a cookie, and Bryn snatched away the pan. "These are for me."

"Not all of them." Maddie clawed the air, coming up empty.

"Yes, all of them." Bryn sifted away, taking the cookies with him.

"Don't worry, Mads, I'll make more."

"You need to train with Excalibur while you have the chance, you know, when you're in between demon hunts."

I picked up my mixing bowl, transporting it to the sink. "I'll get to it soon. I just have so many other things on my mind right now."

She waggled her eyebrows at me. "Yeah, like getting naked with that dragon of yours every chance you get. Don't you think training with Excalibur is more important though?"

I sighed. "Things are just so good between us right now. I want to enjoy it without having to worry about anything else. Because there will be tons of anything else's in the future. Plus, honestly, I'm not sure what I'm supposed to do with Excalibur. Sure, he came in handy with the demon, but I'm not the one who takes care of kills. That's Bryn's job. I'm a unicorn, therefore mostly a pacifist."

Maddie stole a cupcake, grinning at me as she stuffed it in her mouth. Crumbs spilled down her chin as she talked. "There has to be a reason Excalibur claimed you. He wouldn't go to you to sit around collecting dust indefinitely. You need to take the signs into consideration. And I know, you're in your honeymoon stage, I get it, but—"

"Get out. I said the cupcakes weren't ready. You heard me. You were standing right there. And now because you're a pastry thief—no cookies for you."

"Aw, come on, Talia. I just—"

"Nope, none for you." I pointed at the door. I had to keep her and Bryn in line somehow. I'd discovered, much to my delight, that both of them could be swayed with my cooking. It was a bit of a power trip, and I was totally abusing it.

Hmm ... Maybe I'll force them to wear Team Unicorn Talia shirts in order to get any of my delicious food. I chuckled as I pictured it, both Bryn and Maddie looking adorable, I might add. *Yep, should definitely make that one happen.*

Maddie ambled out, her hair hanging in her face. "I'll be back later," she mumbled, shutting the door behind her.

Things were great—practically perfect. And unlike most, I didn't worry about the other shoe dropping when things were in a good spot for me. I enjoyed them while I was there, knowing that if I fell into bad times, the good ones would be just around the corner again. I could get knocked down, just like anyone else, but I would always get up. That was the power of being an optimist.

Bryn sifted back into the kitchen, his gaze darting between the cupcakes and me. When I glared at him, he raised his hands in the air. "I won't take any, I'm not an idiot like Maddie."

A sudden chill raced up my spine, and I stilled, staring blankly at the counter, the marble blurring. But the sensation passed as soon as it started. I rolled my shoulders, smiling. "That was weird."

Bryn brushed my hair out of my face, tucking it behind my ears. "What was that? It didn't feel like a demon."

"It wasn't." I shrugged. "I don't know what it was." Nibbling my lower lip, I turned back to the cupcakes. "It was as if ... I don't know, I can't shake this feeling that I'm forgetting something. Something important."

"If it's important then you probably won't forget it for long. Don't worry." He pressed a kiss to my forehead before scooping me up in his arms. "I know what'll make you forget all about it."

"Forgetting is the problem, Bryn. Are you even listening?"

"Mmm hmm ... something important. I have something important right here."

I giggled. "Stop. I'm serious." But instead of stopping, he swept me away, temporarily erasing all concerns of what I could have possibly forgotten.

Sucks for me that it was something big.

Acknowledgments

I have a whole list of people that deserve to be thanked here, and with that in mind, I was going to simply use my original acknowledgments from the first version of The Trouble with Unicorns buuuut ...I'm currently in the process of moving and all of my books are in boxes. I would rip all those bad boys all open to find my copy of the old The Trouble with Unicorns but let's face it, that seems like entirely too much work and I'm already stressed from all the packing as it is.

I would rather list no one here than risk accidentally leaving someone out. So to avoid such a catastrophe, I'm simply going to thank all of the readers out there that have given my books a chance. You mean the world to me. Thank you.

About the Author

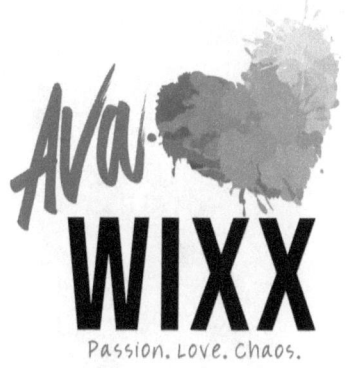

Ava Wixx escaped into books at a young age and decided to stay there. It was only a matter of time before she was driven to create her own fantasy worlds from fear of running out of places to explore.

Reader, writer, dreamer ... Ava only toils in reality when absolutely necessary. She lives in North Carolina with her husband, and spoiled mini-poodle.

(If you want up-to-date info on book-y things then visit Avawixx.com and don't bother with the social media. Because let's face it, Ava is an online slacker and she signed up for some accounts but never actually posts.)